star
bright

ANNE RICHMOND WAKEFIELD

For Steve,
who created time and space—
no small feat.

The cure for pain is in the pain.
—RUMI

Contents

CHAPTER 1

In Raleigh, After

Catherine wants me to write it all down, to tell the whole story: from that first black night on the road, to all that happened next. If I don't write it all down, it's like it never happened. It's like all the pain that scarred me, the miles of darkness and everything, everyone who tried to hurt me, it's like letting them win. I mean, that's not what Catherine said, exactly. She said she wants me to own my story. By capturing it all on these pages, she said, I'll own it.

I get that, I guess. Trapping it on paper should feel less overwhelming, right? I trust Catherine (I guess I should, too, considering how much my stepdad pays her per hour), so I didn't want to tell her that on this point, she's full of shit.

I will always own my story.

It will never leave the marrow of my bones or the veins of my arms. I will never fall asleep or take a shower or drink a glass of water without carrying the full weight of my story. But even Catherine, in all her wisdom, with all the terrible things she's heard throughout her career, she won't get it. She wasn't there.

Lame self-help books talk a lot about integrating trauma into your everyday life. Catherine suggested a few books that encourage this idea. I tried.

I call bullshit.

Anyone who's lived through a trauma knows that it's already knitted into every breath you take.

She nodded when I told her that. She asked what it took for me to survive those bad days.

"What miracles helped you along the way?"

Miracles. That's actually how she talks.

The old me would have ignored her question—insulted it—but I've changed a million times over. After I thought about it a little, I realized a few things got me through. Music, for one, and the birds and animals of the forest. That insistent, unquiet voice inside my head. And learning how to fight.

Although not necessarily in that order.

Afterward, everyone wanted to know everything all at once, which was an impossible weight. I walked around for a few days pressed to the ground, too heavy to think, before Catherine finally said, "Just wait. Tell me your story when you're ready."

No matter what, I own my story. But I know I'm ready to tell it now. It will be imperfect, shaded and torn around the edges. Some of it may not make sense. But it's the truest thing I know.

It was August, a little after nine p.m., and my life finally felt like living when I was yanked out of it somewhere near Asheville, North Carolina. That night I was stolen out of a life that finally felt like something I could live through or, at least, run through. That night, everything changed.

CHAPTER 2

On the Blue Ridge

I whipped open the passenger side door and puked into a row of hedges next to our parking spot. Barely made it to the Mountain Inn, our hotel. The nearest car, a gray station wagon, was a few spots over. The driver was still, her head down almost as if she were praying, so I didn't think anyone saw me.

Disgusting. What's wrong with you? Can't even meet a hot guy without puking.

"Oh my God!" My stepfather Kent shouted, unbuckling his seatbelt and throwing the driver's side door open.

"Are you sick? You can't run sick! Do you have a fever? Let me feel your forehead—"

His pale face was inches from mine, his lip beaded with sweat. I wanted to shove it away.

Get your shit together, Bright. What's that stupid saying? "Fake it 'til you make it"?

Ugh. I grabbed a tissue out of the box on the van's console, shaking back my black hair.

I could tell it was a mess, shaggy and growing out unevenly, and I'd wasted the half hour I'd spent blow-drying it. I thought, suddenly, of the only time a man had ever told me I was beautiful.

I'd been 13 and my math teacher had told me to see him after school. He'd said we needed to talk about my last test, and I'd been terrified. All morning, I'd daydreamed about flight, imagining myself climbing on an airplane, locking and unlocking the tray table as it lifted off the ground, floating away. I wasn't good at math, although no one had seemed to mind. I wasn't good at much of anything except running. It only stung once in a while, a dull arrow in the pit of my stomach.

When Mr. Carson had closed the chalky classroom's door behind me, he'd turned on his heel and faced me. He wasn't tall or short, but he always wore tennis shoes which made him appear out of place among the other laced-up teachers. His hair was fluffy and white as a lamb. He smelled a little like smoke when he leaned toward me, and for a split second, I had no idea what was going to happen.

"You are so beautiful," he'd whispered hotly in my ear. "I'm not sure you even know that, do you? So beautiful."

Pain had welled in my stomach, a hot fountain, and he was kissing my neck. Mr. Carson. Who wore tennis shoes and smelled like dirty cigarettes and was old. Too old to kiss me. I had counted the unsharpened pencils on the desk behind him—one, two, three, all yellow in a line—and then I'd known I was going to throw up.

"I've got to go, Mr. Carson. I'm sick." I'd pulled away.

He had gripped my arm hard. Later, I saw the blue bruise he'd left.

"We can't tell anyone what we've done, okay?" He'd whispered urgently. "We would both be in a lot of trouble."

His eyes were dark gray, creased at the corners. I'd barely heard his last word, "trouble," before I'd leaned over and vomited on his white tennis shoes.

That was four years ago. A lifetime ago.

I shook the memory out of my head, then glanced up at my stepfather's face, etched with more lines than I'd remembered.

"I'm not sick," I said in a low voice, attempting a smile, "but your mountain driving sucks."

Wiping my face with a tissue, making sure there was no puke on my long-sleeved t-shirt or my favorite jeans, I took one more sip of water and stepped through the van door. I heard that voice deep inside my brain:

You don't have to do this. You can go back to Raleigh. Tell Kent you have the flu and you'll never have to face these people.

Kent grabbed my duffel bag from the back of the van. I wished I'd had the extra cash to buy a new bag—this cheap purple and pink one had been in my closet since my Aunt Laura bought it for me when I was ten. I guess I could've asked Laura to buy me a new one. She practically begged to take me shopping before this trip, told me she was treating me because I'd gotten an A on my Spanish test, but I couldn't let her pay for anything else. We'd gotten mani-pedis and waxes after school the day before (she was always telling me, "You can't help being half Cherokee, but I can't let you walk around with a mustache"), so I couldn't ask her for a new bag, too.

You think anyone gives a shit what your nails look like? No one's going to look at you at all.

And I couldn't ask Kent for one more penny. The entrance fee alone for this race was expensive (he'd shaken his head, "I can't believe you have to pay this much for the privilege of running 30 some-odd miles through the wilderness without sleep or real food"), not to mention my share of the rental vans that would drive my team along the course, the motel room I'd be sharing with Tony's wife the night before the race …it was a lot, and I knew Kent was sacrificing to make sure I was able to run it. After all, it had taken a lot of convincing to get Kent to let me go in the first place. "You're always telling me to get more involved," I'd said, "and this is a chance for me to do something new." He argued that it wasn't safe, running in the middle of the night along the Blue Ridge Parkway.

"Kent." I'd said calmly, for some reason not wanting him to understand how important this was to me. "If it wasn't safe, do you really think your friends would want me to do it with them?"

After several conversations with me and phone calls with Darla and Brian, Kent had eventually agreed to let me join the team. But only if I wore my GPS watch. And only if I promised to wear my headlamp and reflective vest the whole time I ran. And only if I called him right after I finished each leg

(I had to break the last promise, it turned out, because cell phone coverage was terrible on the Blue Ridge). Still, I would have promised him just about anything to get to run this relay with Levi.

You can't bail out now.

"Let's go, Kent," I said decisively, pulling at the wrists of my t-shirt. I had to make sure my arms were covered. Always. Didn't want to freak anyone out.

"Hey! Look at that!" Momentarily distracted, Kent gestured toward the sky.

"Impressive, huh?" An enormous hawk, wings spread, glided above us. It reminded me of something I'd read a long time before as I was researching my Cherokee background: that the hawk symbolizes focus and vision. That the Cherokee believe hawks are connected with the spirit world. But even more than that, it reminded me that, although we'd driven here in just a few hours, I was really far from home.

I'd taken one shaky step inside the hotel lobby before I nearly jumped six inches in the air.

"Well, son of a gun!" a booming male voice filled the lobby. "If it isn't Kent-chilada!" From behind a fake fern, I saw my stepdad's friend Tony emerge, all angles and too-short running shorts, drenched in sweat. He embraced Kent, who backed away from him with a chuckle.

"What, Tony, they don't have showers in this place?" Kent's face took on an unfamiliar softness; a look I only saw when he was with one of his friends or reminiscing about the old days. Tony's eyes twinkled in their dark sockets. He was thinner than ever, making him seem older than Kent. His skin was freckled and loosened by the sun, hanging off his cheekbones in tan folds below his jaw. I made a mental note to put on SPF 50 before my day run tomorrow.

"Where's that Bright and Shining Star?" Tony pretended to look past me, shaking out each of his bony legs as he did so.

"I know she couldn't be right next to me. This young lady is far too grown-up to be my little star!"

Jesus. He's as corny as I remember. Let the floor just swallow me up now.

Tony had called me his Bright and Shining Star since I was little. I guessed it was better than what most people called me.

"Hi, Tony." I waved, avoiding touching his sweaty body. He gave me a high five, laughing.

"Where's Darla?" Tony's wife was always easy to talk to.

"She's upstairs with the Moseleys. Levi and I just got back from a run." At the mention of Levi's name, my face got hot. I prayed that neither Kent nor Tony had noticed.

Levi.

You've never even met him, stupid. How ridiculous that you have a crush on him.

My crush on Levi, the college-aged son of Kent's old friends and one of my relay team members, did feel lame. I'd never had a boyfriend or even been on a date. No normal guy—or girl, for that matter—had ever been interested in me. I wasn't sure what made me think Levi would be different. We'd texted some over the past few months, checking in about the race course and worrying about the elevations of our runs.

He seemed really cool, really easy to talk to, as far as guys go. I even Googled him and found his track team photo. He stared out from my screen, blond and sinewy, blue eyes staring right through me. I'd visited that web page a few times a day, each time reminding myself in no uncertain terms that he would never be interested in someone like me. Still, the idea of running in the Blue Ridge Mountains with a really cute, older guy? It made waking up each morning these last few weeks a little easier.

"Bright! Baby!" Darla's gravelly Alabama drawl snapped me back to the present. Thin and tall like her husband, I noticed as Darla walked toward me with arms outstretched that she looked about half her age. Her blond hair, so pale it was nearly white, was pulled back in a sleek ponytail, and she was dressed in black pants. A turquoise tank top exposed sculpted shoulders and arms, and she smiled widely at me.

"Girl, I can't believe it's really you!" she pulled me into an embrace, smelling of grapefruit and nearly bringing tears to my eyes.

She's not your mother.

"You just look so grown-up. I can't wait to get all caught up with you." Darla grabbed both of my hands.

"Kent tells us you are a serious distance runner. I still don't understand why you're not on the cross-country team." Darla seemed to notice me flinch when she said this. Joining stuff was tough for me, which she couldn't have known. Joining a team this year, with everything I'd been through, would have been impossible. She waved her hand, appearing to sweep her comment away.

"We are going to have so much fun!"

And then suddenly he was there. Or had he been there all along?

Levi. He was almost a foot taller than me. He looked older than he had in his online photo and less clean-cut, his hair shaggy and bleached by the sun. I couldn't breathe. I tried to take in his appearance all at once: wide shoulders, legs tanned in his running shorts, thick black tattoo marking the inside of his forearm. I realized I hadn't spoken to him yet, but when my eyes connected with his, I felt like throwing up again.

He's gorgeous. And he will never like you.

"Hey!" he spoke for both of us, his blue eyes dancing. "I'd totally hug you," he smirked a little, "but…" he lifted his soaked gray t-shirt away from his torso, revealing a few inches of tanned stomach muscles.

"So good to finally meet you. How about this place, huh?" he smiled at me, all white teeth and a patch of grizzle under his bottom lip. He talked so fast.

I felt dizzy.

Get it together.

"Oh, yeah," I said. Too loud. "I can't wait to get outside. I need to do a shakeout run today." I shifted my weight from one leg to the other, bouncing slightly on the balls of my feet.

Relax. Lower your voice.

I felt Levi looking at me. He seemed genuinely excited to meet me.

Oh my God.

"So," he took a step toward me, running a massive hand through his wavy blond hair, "I've gotta tell you about this trail we took—"

"I think it's best Bright gets settled," Kent interrupted, looking uncomfortable, the veil of sweat still coating his upper lip. He really didn't look good. He put his arm around my shoulder, pulling me in toward him, an unfamiliar and awkward display of protectiveness. I leaned away from him. "There'll be plenty of time for shakeout runs later, kids."

With Kent's arm around me, I suddenly remembered the last time I'd felt his awkward protectiveness, the last time I'd slept in a bed that wasn't my own like I was about to do. I tried to push away that memory of last year. The sheets there were rough; hospital-issued, smelling of bleach, and better than I deserved. When I woke up, my arms were strapped down to my sides—or that's what I'd thought, initially. In reality, I had IVs dripping fluids and antibiotics into them, and they were wrapped in gauze bandages, burns hidden, two small mummies extending from my body. My first thought when I'd woken up in that hospital bed was of Kent. As tough as things had been in the years since my mother had died, the guilt of forcing Kent to see me in a psych ward, knowing that was where I belonged, knowing it was my fault I was there, made me want to disappear. Kent didn't deserve all that I had put him through. He was a good person, taking me on like he did. I was not his daughter, and I was damaged goods. I'd been so ungrateful.

I couldn't help it. The memory took me over, and tears sprung up in the corners of my eyes. A phantom ache filled my arms, and I wrapped them around my waist.

For God's sake, Bright, control yourself.

I pinched the skin on my stomach as hard as I could, biting back tears.

I looked away from Kent, his arm still draped over my shoulder. My feelings were too much, and I tried to take a deep breath and be in the present moment like Catherine had taught me. I was furious with myself.

"You should go," I tried to keep my voice steady, still looking away from Kent, chewing on my freshly painted thumbnail. My voice sounded angry.

Why are you crying? And nice job ruining your manicure already.

"You're going to hit traffic."

Kent surprised me by taking my chin in his hand and forcing my face toward his. He rarely touched me, other than the occasional, uncomfortable side-hug, seemingly afraid of breaking me or invading my space or offending me somehow. He's not a bad guy, I reminded myself. He's one of the decent ones, he's just so checked out that he can't really be there for anyone. I used to think he'd never remarried after my mom because of me. I figured he didn't want to saddle some other woman with a kid who wasn't even his, let alone hers. I knew I was damaged goods, I'd known it almost from day one, but it turns out he knew he was damaged goods, too. Maybe he never married another woman because he either knew he was too shut down to be a good husband or because he was too absent to ever meet someone. Once I hit high school he could have tried. He occasionally went out with coworkers for drinks after work and he could've looked for another relationship. Aunt Laura tried to convince him to find someone else, not that she was any better than he was. Still, it always seemed to me that Kent was skating over this life, sleepwalking through it, and not really plugged in to anything. He did fine at his job, but never great. He never talked about God or church. I didn't know what he believed in. He hardly read and the only TV he watched was sports, on occasion. Often, at night, he'd just stare into space. I'd come into the family room and he'd be staring at the wall. When he'd see me, he'd give a fake smile, a little embarrassed, and he'd pretend to be doing something else. But I knew he was thinking about my mom.

He looked at me, our eyes nearly level. His lower lip vibrated.

"I'm proud of you, Bright." I was suddenly terrified that *he* would start crying, right then and there, right in the lobby of the Mountain Inn. It was too much. I jerked my chin out of his hand and stepped away from him.

He looked away for a beat, wiping his hands on the sides of his pants.

"You call me when you're finished," suddenly all business. "Don't forget to ice your foot between runs and be sure to drink plenty of water. It may not feel hot outside, but you're going to need it."

My foot. Kent wouldn't stop bugging me about a nagging fascia tear I'd gotten a few months earlier. I'd lied to him every time he asked about it—I don't feel anything when I run on it; I promise—but he'd walked in on me once after I limped home from a long run, wincing through the kitchen for a bag of ice. Kent knew what was up. He'd been a runner, after all, who had pushed through injury and hurt himself permanently. He knew me too well to think I'd drop out of this race because I was hurt, but I guess he figured he'd better at least give me some advice. I nodded at him, not meeting his eyes.

He gave me one last look, unsmiling, and walked away to say goodbye to his friends.

And then he was gone.

• • •

I never got a chance to do a shakeout run, and I was sure I'd never get to sleep after dinner. We ate at the hotel's restaurant, where I sat across from Levi. I barely ate anything—who could eat?—while he inhaled a cheeseburger, fries, and two sodas.

"Does this gross you out?" He'd looked me straight in the eyes, sipping on his Coke. At first, I'd thought he meant the sheer volume of his dinner, and my face must've shown that.

"I mean when other people eat meat in front of you? You're a vegetarian, right?" I was so unused to people knowing (remembering?) details of my life that it took me aback.

"Uh, no." I stammered a little. "It doesn't gross me out. Kent eats meat. I'm used to it."

What a stupid thing to say. Now he knows you never hang out with anyone but your stepfather.

"That's cool. I had a girlfriend who was a total nightmare vegan, you know? No meal without a lecture." He smiled that perfect smile, and I was warmed by the sun.

"I just love animals." I shrugged and tried to smile, and he inexplicably and awkwardly high-fived me across the table. I had to laugh, and fortunately, he did too.

There was nothing to be nervous about; he was easy to be around. He was goofy and a good listener, nodding when it made sense to nod, laughing when I'd hoped he'd laugh. In the middle of telling him the story of how I'd found Flyer, my dog who'd died the year before, it hit me fully: Levi didn't know anything about me. Levi didn't know the kids at school called me Death Wish, or Garbage Girl, or Freak Show; he didn't know me as the messed-up girl, as the anti-social loner who didn't get invited to parties or school dances, the girl who'd set herself on fire and ended up in the psych ward. I could be whatever I wanted because Levi just knew me now; in this moment. In Catherine's words, I could be my authentic self with him. This thought was both liberating and scary as hell because things were about to get really authentic with Levi. Our team was going to run 200 total miles together, over 24 hours, while sharing a van. In spite of all of these thoughts fighting to take over my brain, that night I fell asleep quickly, Darla in the double bed next to me, totally overwhelmed by the day.

It's daybreak and I'm running through the nature preserve behind my house. The air is thick with autumn smells: leaves burning, dampness, the onset of cold. I hear the brush crunch under my running shoes; the wind pulls back my hair. I'm fast. Faster than I've ever been. I'm so fast that it scares me. A flock of large brown birds approaches me, swooping closer and closer to my head. Chasing. I feel afraid, so I run faster. The sun, fat and orange, rises above the hills.

One of the birds swoops in so close to my head I can feel his beak brush my cheek. I scream. I run faster and faster, so fast that I'm about to take flight. So fast, but the bird is faster. I can't escape. He's in my face, picking at my hair—

CHAPTER 3

On the Blue Ridge

"Bright!" A stern whisper had me shooting straight up in my hotel bed.

Darla.

"It's time to get up, sweetie. I think you were having a bad dream."

Her face in the semi-darkness was in mine, lined and almost sinister. I was drenched in sweat and out of breath. Another nightmare. Part of me had thought that removing myself from my old life might also remove my old life from me. No such luck.

I shook my head, hoping to shake the bad dream out of my brain.

"What time is it? Is there coffee?"

Darla laughed, and suddenly she was back to looking like her familiar self.

"Do you think I'd run without coffee? Of course there is." She handed me a cup, then scraped her hair back into a ponytail.

"Get dressed, sweetie. We need to get to the starting line soon."

. . .

It didn't take us long to get ready for our run, just enough time for two cups of coffee and a bagel. I sneakily applied water-proof mascara and a little under-eye concealer when I was in the bathroom (*Why? Like that will help you?*) and it made me feel a little better about how tired I looked. I was nervous about seeing Levi again that morning, I realized. I patted the key pocket of my running shorts and felt the tissue-wrapped razor blades flat against my hip. I didn't expect to need them. I wasn't feeling too anxious that day. But they were there in case I did.

"What's up? You ready?" When Darla and I made it down to the van, my heart jumped at the sight of Levi's face. He had on a loose white tank top and his wild blond hair was pushed back in a stretchy headband. His eyes blazed blue and he nodded when he saw me.

"What is this look? Bjorn Borg at Wimbledon circa 1976?" Shannon, his mother, pretended to be horrified. She was almost as tall as Levi, her dark hair cut into a pixie. "Or did you raid Bright's hotel room for accessories?" I blushed. He just laughed.

"You know I hate tennis. It's all about the 'do, mom. I've got to contain the 'do." He turned to me, unfazed. "We've just got lemon, hope that's okay." He tossed me a bottle of sports drink and leaned against the side of the van.

"Morning, Bright," Brian was jangling the van's keys in his right hand as he stretched his calves, leaning his heels off the curb. Levi's dad was the official captain of our relay team. He was dark haired and delicate and looked nothing like his son.

"I wanted to take a minute to talk to you guys about logistics, okay?"

Levi faced me again. "This dude is the king of logistics."

Brian ignored him. "So, as you know, I've assigned legs to each of the six of us. We'll rotate running throughout the day and night for the next 24 or so hours. Each of us will run three times, and we'll each be running between 30 and 40 miles, total." He paused for a minute. "You're going to be exhausted. You're going to be dehydrated and hungry. You're going to be filthy." He glanced pointedly at Levi. "This is no joke, guys. We are in the Blue Ridge mountains—it's the wilderness here. Hopefully, you all reviewed the websites I sent you and read the information."

Read the information? Yes. I'd absolutely studied it. Knew it backward and forward. *Keep on the lookout for loose dogs and bears. Each runner is required to wear a reflective vest and headlamp, and the relay sponsors are not responsible for any injuries incurred during the race. Absolutely no headphones will be allowed during any runs. No road closures will take place. No team vans will be permitted to follow their racers and obstruct traffic. Be on high alert for cars unused to seeing runners on the treacherous mountain roads.*

And on, and on, and on.

I'd read all the warnings with a pit in my stomach, but at the time the race had seemed so far away that the idea of facing down a wild dog or a bear was absurd.

And yet, here I was.

"I'm less worried about our daytime runs," Brian continued, "but we still have to be vigilant even when it's light out."

He smiled at his son.

"Levi, you're kicking us off this morning. My advice to you? Don't go out too hard. This is the longest total distance you've ever run." He looked around at the rest of us, now really paying attention. "The same goes for all of us, really. We are going to be excited and want to take off. But we'll each be running a lot of mountain miles on very little sleep, and this is not a sprint."

Levi was sitting on the asphalt now, playing with his shoelace. I wondered if he was nervous at all because his face didn't look it. I wondered if he felt like I did: ready to be set free on these roads, ready to go.

Once we drove the van to the race start, Levi still looked calm. I kept trying not to stare at him, but he was a magnet. Tall, tanned, and lean, with an easy smile and that crazy blond hair.

Stop it. Who do you think you are? No way he's going to like you. Just stop.

I'd never seen anything like the scene at the beginning of the race. It was like an out-of-control party at the crack of dawn. You'd never have known that these people were about to run over two hundred miles. Some of the teams were dressed in costumes—one group of women all wore old prom dresses, bright taffeta ruffles swirling in front of a background of sleek runners—and music blared as the orange-shirted volunteers tried to keep everyone under control. It didn't match the majestic beauty of the Blue Ridge Mountains, this raucous laughter and over-the-top humor. I liked it, though. It steadied me. It helped me to remember that the run was about having fun; getting somewhere new. Seeing something different.

Levi caught me looking at the crowd. "They must not be doing the ultra," he nodded toward the costumed women. "Running this thing with a team of 12 people instead of six would be a lot easier." He smiled and winked at me. "But easy's no fun, right?"

"We're all going to cheer Levi on when he starts, but after that, we'll need to get back in the van," Shannon said, looking reluctant. I wondered if she was scared for him, or if she was just envious that he was the runner to kick us off. I noticed Darla put her hand on Shannon's forearm.

"I've got this." Levi flexed his biceps over his head, laughing. I was suddenly overcome with the realization that I was going to be trapped in a van with five other people for the next twenty-odd hours. For weeks, I'd been consumed by the running aspect of this relay; so much so that I'd barely considered the non-running parts.

What in the hell are you going to talk to these people about? How can you possibly spend all this time with Levi without totally losing it?

CHAPTER 4

On the Blue Ridge

I shouldn't have worried. Between runs, the van was quiet. After Levi finished his first eleven-mile leg, which he ran faster than anyone anticipated, Tony (who had been uncharacteristically quiet and focused in the van, reading a book about mindfulness) went out for his. I wished I'd asked for an earlier starting time. I was dying to go.

"Hey." Levi smiled at me, sweaty and sharing my seat. I had my headphones in, listening to old-time music. I didn't know anyone else my age who listened to Doc Watson or The New Lost City Ramblers. I was weird. I knew it. Levi gestured at me to take off my headphones.

"What're you listening to?" he asked, just as I knew he would. I paused for a second.

Lie.

Then Catherine's favorite word—authenticity—rung in my ears. What the hell?

"The Iron Mountain String Band. They play old-time music. Most people our age haven't heard of them." I hated the way my voice sounded; mumbly, superior, and timid all at the same time.

Way to go. From now on, just shut up.

Levi burst out laughing, his salt-streaked face lighting up around the temples.

"You like old time? Bluegrass?"

Suddenly, Brian turned around from his perch in the passenger seat.

"Oh, God, Bright. Don't tell me you are a fan of that hillbilly fiddle music too?" He shook his head in mock disgust. "I forgot to mention the most important rule of this van, kids," he waggled his finger at the two of us in the backseat, "absolutely no banjos. And no music performed by anyone wearing overalls!" He faced forward again, folding a u-shaped travel pillow around his neck.

Levi leaned toward me conspiratorially. "Watch this. He's going to fall asleep in 5…4…3…2…" he nodded in his dad's direction, just as rhythmic snores began.

"Unbelievable."

"I really don't know that much about old time. I'm more into Americana and bluegrass." He paused. "Would you mind?" he gestured at my ear phones, asking if he could listen to one.

Oh my God. He's actually going to listen.

I'd seen it my whole life. Boys and girls sharing a set of ear buds, listening to the same music, enjoying closeness beyond proximity. I'd never shared a set of headphones with anyone.

No friend, no sister, no mother, no one. My stomach flipped and my palms started sweating. I was sitting in the backseat of a van with the hottest guy I'd ever seen, and he was sharing my ear phones. And we'd be by each other's sides for the next 24 hours.

. . .

"Bright! It's time to wake up!"

We had dozed off, Levi and me. Our knees were touching. I had to shake the sleep out of my brain in order to appreciate that fact for one brief and golden second.

Brian patted my shoulder.

"Can't run if you're asleep!" He leaned over me, a damp sweatband across his forehead. The van stunk of feet and body odor. Levi's leg pushed into mine.

I blinked hard, then peered out the van's window. The sun was beginning to set behind the mountains, purpling the sky.

"That's beautiful," Levi murmured sleepily. I imagined he was saying it to me rather than to the sunset.

Focus, Bright. Stop dreaming and prepare yourself.

"I'm almost ready," I pulled my reflective vest out of the overnight bag at my feet. "I need my headlamp, right?"

Brian and Levi both nodded. "It'll be black out there in no time, even with the moonlight and all those stars." Brian shook his head. "On my run, I nearly got pushed off the road by some idiot in a pick-up truck." He pulled a purple towel out of his jacket pocket, wiping his face.

"Please be careful, Bright. This stretch you're running has almost no shoulder. It will be dark. There's a sheer drop off the mountain on the left side, and we're not allowed to follow you in the van…can't block the road." He reached out to me and I flinched a little without thinking. He laughed good naturedly.

"It's not a sprint, okay? Slow and steady."

I nodded.

He doesn't know you.

I'd never run slowly in my life, not even when I'd wanted to. Slow and steady wouldn't happen. Running didn't work unless I was a bird uncaged, an animal set free. My spareness saved me; the angles that kept me a safe distance from desirable helped me cut through the air. I was built to run fast.

"Okay," I said. I knew I should be nervous—running in the pitch black, hillbillies and animals and drunk drivers all around me—but the only flutter I felt in my stomach was excitement. For one thing, my favorite place to run was the sacred, wild space just beyond my suburban neighborhood. Glenlake, as its name states, is bordered on one side by a lake, surrounded by a nature preserve. Gated from the front, the lake seeps out behind Glenlake like an exhalation. In daylight, the preserve's miles of rocky trail are treacherous—there are skunks, raccoons, coyotes, even a bobcat or two—but in darkness? A runner less familiar than I was could easily step off the trail and fall 50 feet into oblivion. So, I have practiced running near ledges, and when I was younger, I thought a lot about falling. On days when the fourth grade encircled me on the playground, calling out my skinny legs or my big nose,

I imagined myself dropping like a stone into that blackness. I didn't *want* to die, but I wondered what it would be like. I eventually decided that falling would be miserable. Because the nature preserve was inaccessible by car, there was a good chance that, if I fell, I'd die of dehydration or exposure, suffering for days before anyone found me. Any search for me would be a tedious one, executed on foot. No one would miss me much anyway.

Also, after everything I had been through in the past year, the relay didn't strike me as the slightest bit nerve-racking. I thought of my conversation with Catherine the previous week.

"Are you afraid of running all of those miles in the middle of the night?" She'd asked, her eyes expressionless. "Is it intimidating to you?"

I hadn't even considered her question before responding. "High school is intimidating to me. Running is freedom."

Now, in the van, Levi looked up at me with a crooked grin on his face.

"I love running in the dark. I'm actually kind of pissed that we have to wear these stupid things." He strapped on his headlamp, trying to make a goofy face but just looking handsome.

When you're running at night, you feel like the only person in the universe; invincible but made of feathers and rubber bands. Strung tight and light as cotton balls. When you're running at night, you are invisible. To make yourself known with a headlamp, a flashlight, a cell phone; that dims the magic a little.

"I totally agree." I cleared my throat. "I went to sleep-away camp when I was little, and I had this counselor who always told us not to turn on our flashlights for night hikes. She said if you just let your eyes adjust, you could see better without a light."

Remember the stars? Remember studying the summer constellations; flashlight under blanket, book open until the counselors made you put it away?

Levi smiled at me and, as corny as it sounds, I really did feel a flutter in my stomach.

"Right? And why didn't I ever get to go to sleepaway camp?" He banged his fist on his mother's headrest.

Shannon popped her head around from the front seat, mock-scowling and reminding me that we weren't alone in the night.

"Because you would've been too homesick. And the only problem with no headlamps? Broken ankles. Or out here, imminent death." She raised one eyebrow. "Right?"

He smiled at his mom, and I tried not to stare. The forced intimacy of the van was like nothing I'd ever experienced before. It was unfamiliar, but I thought I could get used to it. Sitting next to Levi, sharing earphones in the dark, smelling him, hearing Tony and Darla breathe in unison, sleeping next to each other, being privy to intimate conversations…I tried not to let myself get overwhelmed by the moment, but to instead remember it, live it fully enough that I could pull it out like a photograph on those inevitable dark future days when I couldn't sleep, when I felt the world folding in on me.

What's in the air? What does it smell like, feel like, taste like?

I committed Levi's salty musk odor to memory. The press of his leg against mine. I took a deep breath.

"We're here, Bright. Get ready to run."

I pulled out my earphone and glanced at Levi.

"Nervous?" He rubbed my shoulder. I was electric.

I shrugged and let him walk me out of the van. It was almost dark, and Levi looked up at the sky, his throat golden in the dying light.

"Check it out. 'Star light, star bright, first star I see tonight.' C'mon now. Make a wish, Star Bright."

I groaned quietly. Was he making fun of me, or did he just give me a nickname?

"Jesus, cynical much?" He pointed up, and sure enough, there was a point of light in the still-blue sky.

I laughed.

"I guess I can be." I liked that he called me out. I liked even more that he didn't seem the slightest bit self-conscious about his corniness. "Okay, I'll play. So, what are you going to wish for?"

"What? Oh, hell no. If I told you, it wouldn't come true. Just let your head get wet with the midnight sky." He winked and smiled at me, sending chills up and down my spine. He was quoting old-time music, but I realized that getting my head wet with sky was exactly what I wanted. I just wanted him with me when I did it.

Make a memory. Once he figures out how lame you are, this won't ever happen again.

"And go run your ass off."

"Don't worry," I said before I could stop myself. "Don't worry about me for a second." I wasn't sure why, but it seemed like the right thing to say. I smiled. He smiled back.

. . .

SESSION #: 1
DATE: JUNE 27
TIME: 9:30 A.M.
CATHERINE M. SONDLER, LCSW

Client presented as clean, oriented to her surroundings, and well-nourished. Client is a 52-year-old Caucasian female with dark brown hair. No obvious physical disabilities. Presenting problems included bipolar disorder, anxiety, and depression. Referred by primary care physician.

Initial interview revealed a history of childhood displacement and chaos. Client shared that she lived in multiple foster homes from the age of three to the age of 13. Intermittently returned to her family of origin, which included a father who abused alcohol and six younger siblings. Reported physical abuse from father and sexual abuse from multiple foster parents but stated she "doesn't really remember it." No education beyond seventh grade. Reported first pregnancy at the age of 14. No prenatal care. Infant died at three days old of unknown causes. Reported second pregnancy at age 16 resulting in stillbirth. No prenatal care. Client stated she "lost her mind" after stillbirth, stating she walked "miles and miles along the road near my cabin...people thought i was blind because I couldn't look at anyone or anything." Suspected grief-related psychotic break. No previous psychiatric treatment.

Client stated that during this time she began working with a volunteer mentor. Stated her father was resistant to mentor's involvement, but that ultimately the mentor's financial help "saved the family." Stated that mentor helped her find grief counseling, tutoring, career counseling leading to technical college, health and dental care, and heating system for cabin. Indicated that mentor saved her life and became tearful to the point of inability to speak when sharing about mentor.

Discussion with client about treatment goals. Managing anxiety and grief symptoms are primary goals, as are developing increased coping skills and tolerance for distress. Assigned client journaling homework. Next session scheduled.

CHAPTER 5

On the Blue Ridge

The sun was almost gone. As much as I tried to run easy at first, I couldn't help myself. All the energy and nervousness and anticipation of this race were stored in my legs, and I felt like I'd shatter into a million pieces if I didn't run some of it out.

The Blue Ridge was the most beautiful place I'd ever seen. The mountains rose before me like something out of a fairytale, teal and purple in the dusk. Pine trees that would stand decorated in living rooms in a few months dominated the distance, and the light from the setting sun painted everything in gold shimmer. Something welled up in me as I started to run, that feeling like sadness (or longing?) wrapped in a veil of euphoria, and I couldn't hold back my tears.

Why in the hell are you crying?

If I'd learned nothing else over the past year, I knew that crying was okay. I knew, logically, that expressing emotion was the goal: that crying over a breathtaking landscape meant

I was touched by beauty; that I was living honestly. So why did I still feel ashamed? I remembered when I first started meeting with Catherine how I was so shut down I could barely talk to her. Instead, I handed her a journal entry that said, *"Nobody knows me at all. I don't want anyone to know me—I don't want to be opened up and laid bare to kids at school, to teachers, to my family. I already get made fun of enough for what they assume about me. How ripped open, how dissected would I be if they saw through the cover? If everyone pulled aside the curtain of my hair and peeked into my eyes, if they saw the blood and the fire, the damage, the ugliness, what then? How much worse would it get? I know what you're going to say. Something like, 'Being known can be liberating. No matter what you may believe about yourself, we all—humans—have a drive to be known, to be understood. Even though you don't think you need people, how much better would you feel if you were known...scars and all?'*

I imagine you saying that to me because, well, you may have already said it. And it isn't untrue. It's telling the truth after a long lie. It's shrugging your shoulders and saying, 'Like it or fuck off.'

So, then, what happens when everyone would actually rather fuck off?

I've never learned the answer to that question because I've never cracked myself open when other people are around."

I'd reread that journal entry right before leaving for the relay. The closest I'd ever come to cracking myself open was this relay which, let's face it, was going to leave me pretty vulnerable. It felt perfect, though, for me to do the one thing I'm really good at with people who have no reason not to like me.

And now here I was, crying and running on a mountain road.

Sure hope Levi can't see your face.

But, of course, he couldn't. As promised, the van had taken off as soon as I started running. Brian had said they'd try to wait for me a couple of miles up the road to give me a water bottle. That didn't matter to me. All I cared about was moving forward. And I didn't want to hurt myself; to numb my tears with blood.

No one else is here. You're the only person left in the world. Just how you like it.

Because there were so few teams running the relay, I'd read that it wasn't uncommon to run for miles without coming across another runner. I'd also read that it was pretty easy to get lost along the course. Marking off 200-plus miles of road is a big job, and the volunteer staff was small. So, I tried to keep a solid pace but stay aware of my surroundings. I'd studied maps of the race course—I'd even tacked one to the wall beside my bed so that I could look at it as I fell asleep—but I knew I couldn't get too comfortable.

Keep breathing.

It got dark fast. I managed to turn on my headlamp and attach it to my forehead without slowing down even a little bit. I was aware of the road ahead of me, but soon enough I understood how easy it would be to take one wrong step and fall off the mountain.

Focus, Bright. Concentrate on your steps.

Glancing down at my watch, I saw that it was 7:48.

I heard the rumble of a vehicle behind me, accompanied by shouts. My van.

Levi rang a cowbell out the side window, grinning widely. "You're killin' it, Bright! Way to go! Need anything?"

I shook my head. *Just you,* I thought to myself, then blushed.

"Okay!" Levi shouted again, "Only 14 uphill miles to go in the dark! Nothing fun about easy! We'll see you at the exchange zone!" The words fell out of his mouth and then his golden head was back in the van. The vehicle rumbled ahead of me on the narrow road, Darla's white head behind the wheel, and a part of me was happy. I didn't want to be watched. I would do what I did best, I'd run hard, following the directions printed on the index card Brian had handed me earlier until it was time to pass my official wrist band to the next runner at the exchange zone.

Something skittered right in front of me on the road…A rabbit, maybe? I jumped, trying not to lose my footing.

Just a bunny, stupid. Keep your head up.

I looked to my right and saw what looked like a ramshackle house; its porch light illuminated paint-peeled shutters and a washer and dryer on the sagging front porch. The scent of cigarette smoke made its way to my nose, causing a wave of nausea. I saw an old man sitting in a plastic deck chair on the porch, staring me down as he sucked on his cigarette. I felt a flash of vulnerability, reminded that I was on my own on this road. The hair on the back of my neck rose. The man smiled at me. I didn't smile back.

"Be careful out there!" he shouted after me, after I'd gone. I felt guilty for not having been friendlier but didn't have much time to dwell on that feeling before I heard the frantic, throaty barking of a dog. Out of nowhere, it bounded up to me and I forced myself not to panic. He's just like Flyer, I told myself. Nothing to be afraid of. As the dog got closer I saw his tail was wagging and his teeth weren't bared. As sinister as he had sounded in the darkness, he was just a sweet Lab up close.

Let that be a lesson, Bright.

I couldn't be slowed down, though. The dog followed me, tail wagging, for a few yards before losing interest and running back home. And like always, I got into a rhythm. I went to that headspace that's kind of like meditation; a zone-out place where I felt in charge. Such a stark contrast to how I felt walking through my day. I lost time, a little. I let the darkness hypnotize me. No headlights. No light at all, except for the shine from my headlamp, just ahead of my running shoes.

And then, I wasn't alone.

I felt the car before I saw it. The road almost pulsed with its whine. It wasn't the team van. It sounded smaller; its noise higher pitched.

Don't turn around. Just keep running.

I sped up, but the car slowed down. The road narrowed into scarcely two lanes, and I heard the car humming right behind me.

It's only slowing because it doesn't want to scare you.

I looked at my watch: 9:02. Still early. Nothing bad happened that early.

The driver tapped its horn. Its stark beep ripped open the mountain quiet. I was annoyed. What in the hell could this guy want?

Just face forward. Just keep running.

Sweat prickled under my arms despite the cool night temperature, and in my peripheral vision, I saw the car pull up beside me.

"Hey, honey!" It was a woman's voice, not nearly as threatening as I'd thought. But I wouldn't slow down.

I turned to look at her for just a second, returning my eyes to the road as soon as possible.

Round face, glasses, frizzy blond hair, overweight. Totally nonthreatening.

"'Scuse me, honey?" her voice was high pitched, childlike. "I can see you're running here. I live just a little bit back that-a-way, and I'm a volunteer for the race. I'm Lorraine."

I kept my eyes on the street in front of me but imagined she was gesturing behind her with one hand. Her car crawled alongside me.

"I already called the sheriff." The word startled me. I glanced at her again. Light car—grayish—that had seen better days. Some kind of hatchback or station wagon. It looked familiar, and then I remembered having seen it in the hotel parking lot when I'd gotten sick. It was the praying woman. More importantly, she was wearing the bright orange shirt, announcing "VOLUNTEER" across her chest, that all the others working at the starting line had been wearing.

"The sheriff hasn't come out yet. I saw the bear right alongside the road yonder, and that means he's likely headed this way."

The bear. Oh God.

We knew this was a possibility from the beginning, of course. These were the Blue Ridge Mountains, after all, and they belonged to the bears, not to the ultra-runners. All the materials from the race and the website warned about being mindful of wildlife. Brian had even emailed us all an article about how East Coast black bears, once considered nonaggressive, had been attacking humans more frequently as we encroached on their territory. Still, I guess I just didn't anticipate it actually happening.

I slowed down a little.

"A bear?"

"Get in the car, hon," she commanded. "You ain't gettin' paid to run, are you?" She giggled, sugary and girlish.

I shook my head, irritated. I was torn. Getting into the car meant I was cheating. Although my team wasn't expecting to win the relay, and there was no prize for winning anyway, I'd never cheated on or been disqualified from anything in my life. I'd never given up on running. But, this was a bear. I was all alone in the wilderness. The sheriff was coming.

"Just until they trap him," she said, reading my mind. "Then, I'll drive you right back to this spot, so you can keep on. It won't be like you are cheating or nothin'." She smiled at me, I noticed from the corner of my eye.

"I've been volunteering for this race long as they've been doing it. They'll believe me when I tell 'em about the bear." I slowed down more, considering my options.

Let down your team by getting into a car. Or get eaten by a bear.

What would Catherine say?

She'd say, "Trust your gut."

I took a deep breath and began to walk. "Okay, then. Just until they catch the bear."

The woman smiled, then leaned over to unlock the passenger door for me. She extended a plastic bottle of water to me in her hand, which had torn cuticles and dirt under the nails. I didn't want to insult her. I was thirsty. I took the bottle and gulped half of it, feeling it make its way from my lips to the pit of my stomach in a way I'd never noticed water go down before.

Her car was filthy inside. The smell hit me first; it stunk of mold and cigarette smoke. There were papers and empty soda cans, saltine cracker boxes, and snack cake wrappers all over the floorboards where my feet should be, and I kicked them without meaning to.

"Sorry," I mumbled. "Thanks for picking me up…Lorraine."

She smiled. "You need to drink, hon. Can't be dehydrated out here." She sang the last part, nodding at me. She sped up around a turn, which didn't seem right.

Nothing seems right.

The car was too hot. She clicked the locks and, I realized, it was an older car with those bar locks that disappeared into the doors. I put my hand over it, but I couldn't grip the lock.

The car was so cluttered. Did she live in it? I glanced into the backseat. Full black garbage bags lined the floorboards. Then, on the rear console, I saw it: an ax. I turned back around to face her.

What have you done?

Jesus, what have you done?

It was so hot. I was so tired, and I reached out my arm toward Lorraine, but I felt like I was trapped inside a bubble of hot steam. I tried to talk but my mouth wouldn't work. The car sped up and she smiled at me again. My eyelids were so heavy. "Just sleep now, Natalie. You rest your head. It's going to be a long night."

. . .

There was music. The melody was faint; circling my memory. It was an old hymn my mother used to sing to me when I was little.

Bright morning stars are rising

Bright morning stars are rising

Bright morning stars are rising

Day is a-breaking in my soul...

My mom was walking toward me, a gentle smile on her face as she sung, low and sweet. I tried to stand up, to greet her, to embrace her, but my legs were frozen and my body was paralyzed.

My mom stopped singing and spoke to me. Her hair shone and I could see her small gold earrings glowing in her earlobes.

"You probably don't know this, but I always thought I would name you Hailey. *Hailey.* The way the syllables roll between the tongue and the teeth, the long 'A' sound, it just feels like sunshine. A little girl named Hailey, I always thought, would have shiny hair and shoulders full of freckles. A girl named Hailey would catch lightning bugs in the summer and make snow angels in winter. She'd fix her hands on her hips when lit up with righteous indignation. Your father, for what it's worth, loved the name, too. He insisted on your middle name—Camila—after his mother, long dead from a car accident but on a pedestal in his childhood memory."

She was singing again.

Oh, where are our dear fathers?
Oh, where are our dear fathers?
They're down in the valley a-praying
Day is a-breaking in my soul

"You probably don't know that you were two days from being born when your father disappeared. Disappeared, as in left-his-work-boots-on-the-back-porch-and-never-came-for-them vanished. Vaporized, first a cloud of pipe smoke and an easy smile and then...nothing. He went to work at the same restaurant where he'd clocked in, sober and shining like a sink, every day for the past five years. He never came home. I panicked at first, of course. I worried that he'd met a knife in the alley or worse, and then I remembered: I'd resigned myself, long before the day he disappeared, to a life of suffering in exchange for you. I wanted you more than I deserved to hope. I gave up your father because I wanted you more, and I need you to know that."

Her hair hung thick to her shoulders like it had before she got sick. She was so beautiful. My mother. My heart was in my throat.

Oh, where are our dear mothers?
Oh, where are our dear mothers?
They've gone to heaven a-shouting
Day is a-breaking in my soul
And her voice again.

"The day you were born, I was alone in my skin. My mother never liked me much and my father, as you know, died of cancer too young. Like I did. You slipped into the world like you owned it, a fire in your eyes and skin too dark for a Hailey. The name was too small for a spirit that burned so bright—from the first breath you took. When the nurse asked me, alone in my hospital bed, no husband, no mother, no one, what your name was, my brain was feathery from exhaustion, my muscles twitching. I thought of a hymn my father used to sing to me—not sure how it clawed through the swarm in my brain, but figure it climbed out for a reason—and I smiled up at the nurse. 'Bright.' I said. 'That's her name.'"

I tried to call out to her, but my dream-voice wouldn't cooperate. The song got softer and my mother's voice rose like a cloud before me, floating away.

Oh, Mom. You climbed out for a reason. Stay.

CHAPTER 6

On the Blue Ridge

You're alive. Just barely.

My head felt cleaved in two, cracked open like a jack-o-lantern. Everything was black. Was it pain squeezing the sunlight from my eyes? Something else?

I smelled morning, through a hot black haze. Damp grass, pine needles, mildew, smoke. In my brain, my blood-red brain, I felt morning.

And I was moving forward, one foot before the other. How? I was being dragged. Someone was dragging me, pulling me by my wrists. Panic grabbed my stomach. I tried to breathe.

You're walking. Keep walking. You're breathing. Keep breathing. Stay upright.

Breathing in. Something was covering my mouth, hot over my eyes, oh GodGODGODGod, please take this pain away. (But God was never where I needed Him, was He?)

Keep moving. Keep walking. Keep breathing.

"Step slowly, honey."

I put one foot in front of the other. I had to. I'd fall otherwise. Out of the blackness, there it was: a voice so close I could feel its breath. It was sweet. The sound pumped adrenaline into my joints; made me ready to run. My feet drag-crunching along what felt like a gravel path, the air was a blanket, warm and wet. My underarms were damp with sweat.

Keep moving. Keep breathing.

"Lots of roots here, maybe even a frog or a snake."

The voice again. It was feminine and kind. I remembered Lorraine.

Oh my God, you remember! Where are you?

Don't panic. Keep breathing.

If it's morning, why's it black?

Keep walking.

More sweat in the corners of my eyes. Stinging. I needed to wipe it, but I couldn't move; I was like a dog being led by my wrists. Like a dog on a leash. My stomach flipped. I breathed in so sharply it hurt.

You can't move your hands!

"I can't move my hands," I shouted, shocking myself. My voice was raw, red like my brain.

Something—a cord, a rope—dug into my wrists, where the scars are the worst, forcing my shoulders forward.

"What the hell is happening?"

My upper arm. She'd grabbed me. The hand felt too cold for the smothering air. The skin was rough, like too many dishes or no winter gloves.

"Language!" Lorraine sing-songed and then grabbed my face with those rough hands, the way you'd pinch a toddler's chubby cheeks.

I was sick, suddenly. Breathing in hot air, I thought I might throw up.

No one helps sick. People help pretty, sweet, soft. You need help. Keep breathing. Be nice. Be nice.

"Um, excuse me? Lorraine?" I was too polite.

I tried to clear my throat. I was going to puke. Brain burning, I talked louder.

"Lorraine...where are we? Tell me why you are doing this. Please?"

My words hung. I saw them, hanging on the edge of the darkness. I was still walking. My right sock soaked through and warm. Sweat? Blood?

The voice laughed, melodious and sunny.

"Oh, Natalie," it giggled, its hand now gently stroking my short ponytail. "Stop being so silly. We're outside, of course. We're on our way into the cabin. There's nothing to be afraid of. You're with me—your Mama."

CHAPTER 7

In Raleigh, Before

"After your mom died, you said Kent's sister was around a lot. Did you feel like your aunt stepped in as a mother figure?" I noticed Catherine seemed to want me to have a mother figure, but Aunt Laura wasn't exactly that.

"Well, I always feel like I can ask her anything. Doesn't mean she'll answer, but she's honest with me."

All that was true. But when she's had a few drinks, Laura's more than honest and that's usually as much as I can handle. I remember Aunt Laura being around from the beginning: when my mom was sick, it was always Laura who was making dinner for me, Laura driving me to and from school, Laura tucking me into bed at night. She was the one who signed my permission slips and bought me underwear. She did all the things a mother does for her child, but she wasn't a mother figure. She isn't. I love her, but I feel a little sick when Catherine asks me about Aunt Laura "stepping in." For years, I thought Laura lived with us because at night she'd most often collapse on the couch after she put me to bed. This was mostly because there was no one waiting for her at home.

"Did you ever stay at your aunt's place?"

I nodded. "Sometimes. Especially when I was little."

I loved her apartment. It wasn't too far from us but felt like a world away. It was safe. Colorful and warm. She had a turquoise leather sofa and red velvet throw pillows, tapestries hanging on the walls and antique mirrors in her bedroom. Her paintings lined the hallways throughout the place.

"But she drinks too much, you've said. Is that why you didn't stay with her when you were older?"

"She's not a mean drunk or anything," I felt a little defensive, even though Catherine was right—as usual. "She's not belligerent or angry when she drinks, but I guess I don't like it."

I'd seen Laura one too many times after about three too many glasses of wine, and it made me feel, I don't know, unsafe. I didn't want to talk to Catherine about this, though. I didn't want to think too much about it, even, but I couldn't help myself. I mean, I get that Laura feels misunderstood by a world she entirely misunderstands—she is an introvert and an artist who would much rather spend her days locked in her studio than teaching undergraduates and lecturing at a university. She's told me before how it drains her; how the endless standing and talking and interacting with her students feels like a literal sap on her energy; how at the end of the day she can barely change her clothes before she falls into bed. I think she's exhausted by the efforts of pretending to be normal. Kind of like me, maybe, if I tried. Her drinking is my cutting, so I get it. I also get why it terrifies me and why I don't want to be around it.

If I'm really honest, I guess I was, and still am, simultaneously drawn to and repelled by my aunt when she's drinking. When it was really late and she was really loosened up she would occasionally talk about Denny. He was her first husband from when she was young and an art student living in New York.

"He was beautiful," she's said, many times. "You've never seen a man so beautiful." And next, with a wink, "You know, I wasn't too bad to look at back then, either."

The one time I tried to ask Kent about Denny he cursed and said he hoped that bastard was rotting in hell where he belonged.

"What do you mean?" I remembered asking, innocent. "I thought they were in love." I'd always figured he'd died in some tragic accident or, like my mom, was stolen young by cancer.

"You know that scar on Laura's chin?" Kent's eyes were blazing. I'd never seen him like that before. I nodded. The scar was an inch-long thickened stripe where everything else was smooth.

"He gave that to her the last time he beat her up. I thought my dad..." Kent shook his head and started to censor himself before realizing that this story might actually serve as some sort of lesson to me. "I thought my dad was going to kill that man when he saw Laura's face. He took the train up to New York after she ended up in the hospital. You wouldn't believe that asshole. Draped over her hospital bed and crying that he was sorry."

Kent had looked down and said, "She'd believed Denny every other time he'd said that to her. But that day, when Dad reached over and grabbed him by the scruff of the neck like the dog that he was, Denny hauled back and punched Dad in the jaw."

I'd gasped a little, encouraging Kent. "Oh, yeah. Dad saw stars for sure. Can you believe that? Who cold cocks an old man in a hospital room?" He answered his obvious question. "That Denny. The same asshole who beats up his girlfriend who's a hundred pounds soaking wet."

Kent had paused and, I think, he'd believed he'd said too much. He hadn't, of course. That conversation had been a window into who Kent had been before my mother's death had floored him; who he might have been without me around. After that conversation, any time Laura brought up Denny all I could see in my mind's eye was a long-haired hippie guy with bright blue eyes cold-cocking her dad. Because I'd only seen one photo of Kent and Laura's father, the one taken at my mom and Kent's wedding, in every daydream I had old Max was wearing a tuxedo. I don't remember Max from the wedding, of course, because I was so little. But I always heard stories from Kent about what an honorable man he was; a veteran, a fisherman, an attorney. When his name came up in conversation, Laura usually left the room. In years past I hadn't known why, but I'd assumed she was grieving and sad at the loss of her father. Max had died not long after my mom and Kent married, apparently, and that's all I knew of him. Even when she'd been drinking, Laura had never mentioned her father.

I thought about Catherine's question again, wondering how long I'd sat in silence, revisiting memories of Laura I was too uncomfortable to share. What in the hell was a "mother figure," anyway? I loved Aunt Laura, and she was complicated. I trusted her to a degree, but neither my love nor my trust was without conditions. She wasn't my mother. For some reason, the fact that Catherine was even asking me to compare Aunt Laura to a mother, to *my* mother, made me furious. I pinched the skin in between my thumb and pointer finger as hard as I could, keeping the angry tears back. When I knew I could speak again, I did.

"Look, Laura's not my mother, okay? She's nothing like my mother."

CHAPTER 8

On the Blue Ridge

After what sounded like some fumbling with keys and the scrape of metal on metal, an ear-splitting creak made me jump. Lorraine gave me another tug and the ground under my feet changed; it was more solid. The air felt cool around my face, drying the sweat under my eyes and on my chin. It smelled musty. Judging from the stillness of the air and the scent of something human, I was indoors. The faint scent of sweat, the tang of body odor, the slight undercurrent of soap. Lorraine's smell. My smell.

Where are you?

Knowing I was inside, I couldn't get my bearings. She'd put that black thing over my face, so I couldn't see. My head pounded with a ferocity I'd never felt before. I heard the creak again, and then the slam of a heavy door. The metallic scrape, what must have been a lock, once more.

"Please," I murmured. "Please let me uncover my face. I'm so hot. I'm having a hard time breathing." That wasn't exactly true. Since we'd come inside, the stillness of the indoor air had cooled me a bit. I also guessed the sun had been beating down on my face when I was outside. I was able to breathe okay. I just wanted to see where I was.

She laughed.

Why is she always laughing?

"Silly Natalie," her voice trilled, "you can breathe just fine." She sighed. "But, I guess it's time to eat. Are you hungry?"

I didn't know what time it was. I took a deep breath and tried to tune in to my stomach.

"Yes." My voice sounded parched. I'd have done anything to get that cover off my head.

"All righty, then," And suddenly my head was filled with blistering light as she ripped off the black bag. I cried out.

"Such dramatics, Natalie." She made a clucking sound and shook her head. "Never remember you being this dramatic before."

And her face was in mine: frizzy blond hair and a round face out of focus. Dizziness overwhelmed me as I scanned the room. It looked like a regular cabin; its walls were wooden logs. I didn't see any windows, although there must've been some to let this light in. I was blinded. My head felt broken. There was no other word for it.

"My name is Bright," I said, my voice foreign.

Her hand stroked my hair again, harder this time, and then she yanked it. Hard.

"Did those people teach you to be disrespectful, Natalie? Did they teach you to contradict your mama?"

I shook my head, not realizing her hand was still grabbing my hair. I must've winced.

"Don't like that too much, do ya honey?" Her voice. It was familiar, yet so terrifying. She sounded like a horror-movie doll come to life.

"I'm not sure what kind of haircut this is, anyway," she muttered under her breath, and I was aware again of my chopped-off hair, cut off in my old life, the life I left behind. I fought tears.

Get it together, Bright. For God's sake, suck it up.

"No ma'am." I couldn't remember the last time I'd called anyone ma'am. It was probably in the second grade when my teacher demanded it of us.

"Well, that's good. Go wash up now. Dinner soon." She gestured across the room to a wash basin that looked like it had been around since the pioneer days. Everything in the cabin, I realized, was spotless. The floor, where I sat, was swept even though it was rotting in sections. I craved water from the immaculate wash basin but rising to my feet was a more difficult task than I had anticipated. The cabin tilted and the walls shifted, and I fell. My foot, the injury I'd been hiding from Kent for months, flamed with pain.

"Oh, clumsy Natalie," Lorraine sighed heavily, bending at the waist and hoisting me by my underarms. "Upsy daisy." She was stronger than she looked, lifting me like I was a toddler.

I managed to limp to the wash basin, pour in water from a red pitcher, and soap my face. There was no mirror, a fact for which I was glad. The soap stung my face, and I was aware

I must have cuts all over it. I started to pour water from the pitcher directly into my mouth, but Lorraine yelled at me, "Manners!" I was so thirsty. Without warning she was next to me, thrusting a cold bottle of water in my hand and urging me to drink it. Letting the water fill my body, imagining it resuscitating my dried-up stomach, kidneys, liver, I didn't think.

When the bottle was drained, I looked up at Lorraine—I felt I knew her but couldn't place her—and my stomach filled with a familiar warmth.

"Oh…again. Again." I tried to say more but my brain and mouth wouldn't cooperate.

"You drugged me again?!" I couldn't be sure if I'd said the words out loud or just in my head, because before I knew it, my knees buckled, and the world went black once more.

Chapter 9

In Raleigh, Before

"Tell me what things were like after your mom died," Catherine had asked. "What did you do?" She'd leaned back in her chair slightly, expectantly. I'd taken a deep breath.

"I don't know."

"You don't know? You don't remember what it was like?"

I'd exhaled.

"I don't know. It sucked."

She should have been frustrated with me, but Catherine didn't act like she was. She just sat there, not saying anything, until the silence got so uncomfortable I felt like I had to break it.

"I mean, I guess Kent sort of decided he should act like a real father and take care of me. Or maybe he just wanted me out of the house for a while so he could stare at the walls without me staring at him. Whatever. So, he signed me up for this camp, Camp Sunshine, a week of sleepaway camp dedicated to 'helping youngsters grieve the loss of an important person.'"

I'd paused, a little impressed that I remembered the camp's motto.

"What was it like?"

"I mean, it was okay."

Again, with the long pause. Catherine was good at this.

"Well, they told me my mother died because a disease stopped her heart from beating and her lungs from working."

I didn't feel like talking to her. God, did I not feel like it. Talking made me remember. I remembered how the counselors told me that even though she was no longer with me physically, my mother would live on in my memory. How they told me death wasn't like a vacation; that once my mom died, she wouldn't come back from being dead.

"And what did you think about that, when you were seven? How did that make you feel?"

I'd given Catherine a *"Seriously?"* look since we'd already talked about how annoying I find the clichéd therapist question. I'd sighed, I think. I remember sort of resigning myself to the conversation.

"Well, Kent had barely talked about my mother's cancer at all." It was true: She had sometimes tried to tell me she was dying, but when she talked about "going to be with Jesus" I hadn't understood. I certainly hadn't imagined her looking like she did near the end—dry lips, gray face, half-closed eyes. That confused me.

Catherine nodded.

"Camp Sunshine cleared some things up for me, I guess. It also let me meet other kids whose parents had died."

"Did you make friends?"

I nodded, remembering. "This girl Samantha was about my age."

"At camp, there was always a 'question of the day' before Circle Time. Something like, 'What's the hardest thing about losing your loved one?' Or 'What would you tell your loved one if he or she were sitting here today?'"

I stopped for a second, remembering. On that day, the question had been, "What do you miss most about your loved one?" and Samantha's answer was, "Her smell." I'd totally gotten it. In fact, the thing I missed most about my mom was her smell, too. I couldn't say it after Samantha, of course, because then I would've looked like I was copying. So, I'd said her smile. And that was true, too. I missed it all. I gave up trying to count the things I missed.

"Samantha and I had stuff in common."

"It must have helped to have someone you connected with."

I nodded. "Camp Sunshine was good. It was a chance to, I don't know, to breathe." Even as a little kid, when I was at home with Kent, I felt like I was suffocating in our dirty house. I mean, my mom was never much of a clean freak, and she'd been too sick to do anything for a long time. Kent was trapped in his sadness, unavailable in every important and unimportant way. I was miserable, and things felt chaotic. At camp, life was orderly.

"Things were organized. I could also ask the questions I needed to ask and actually get answers."

"Like?"

"Like," I took a breath myself, "did my mom feel pain in the end?" (No, they told me, she was on a morphine drip.) I'd also asked, "Did my mom regret leaving without saying goodbye?" (Yes, the counselors assured me. Of course she did), "Could my mom think after she was dead?" (This one was trickier. Some said dead was immobile and without feelings, without thought. Some said we don't know for sure.), And the toughest question, the one that kept getting stuck painfully in my throat; so hard to ask and so critical, "Was it my fault?"

The day I'd finally gotten up the courage to ask that one, I'd asked it of a counselor named Britt. She had white-blonde hair and freckles, and I watched the inner rims of her eyes go red when she heard me. She took my chin in her hand, which struck me as a gesture someone much older than she was would have made, and looked me straight in the face.

"No. It was cancer's fault. You were her light." I could barely hear her voice, she'd spoken so quietly. I knew both because she worked there and because of the quiver in her voice that she'd lost someone important, too. I let her hug me. After that, I don't remember anyone hugging me for a long, long time. You know what I always remembered, though? "You were her light."

CHAPTER 10

On the Blue Ridge

This is surreal. This isn't happening. You can't actually be here. Where are your teammates?

A knot in my chest. A fist of pain.

Levi.

My vision was slowly coming back, but my mouth felt like it was filled with cotton balls. I lifted myself up on my elbows. Lorraine had just left me, her beloved "daughter," like a pile of dirty laundry on the floor. Like a pile of garbage.

My thoughts immediately turned to the van, to Levi's smile, to Darla. The lump from my chest rose to my throat as I tried to orient myself. I realized the team might not even know I was gone yet. Did they think I was still running?

Where are you? Before you do anything else, figure out where in the hell you are.

I tried to be subtle, not wanting to call attention to the fact that I was checking out my surroundings, so I kept my hands cupped around my eyes as I looked around the room. I felt dizzy, so I closed one eye for a while.

One room. Ancient wooden floor. Small kitchenette in one corner, featuring a mini-fridge and a two-burner stove. No mirrors anywhere. One neat green cot; a pillow with a Hello Kitty pillow case. One sleeping bag on the floor.

Strangely reinforced door with a giant metal bolt across its length. Locked. Everything else looked clean but shabby, decrepit, falling apart. The door looked brand new.

You're never going to get out of here.

Now a red ribbon of panic rose in my chest.

"I need to go to the bathroom," I said, using my elbows to sit up straighter, and I hoped it was true. If I didn't need to pee, I was dangerously dehydrated. My head was swimming, the lights wearing halos and a sour taste rising in the back of my throat.

Lorraine sat at the small table glaring at me, a brown mug of something in front of her. "You need to go to the bathroom, *what?*" she sang.

I took a deep breath. "Please."

"You need to go to the bathroom, *what?*" This time, her voice had an edge; it was even higher pitched.

"Please," I said. A please so full of hope and desperation, so full of sadness. "Mama."

I looked at her face, which had a little satisfied smile. I wanted to smash my fist in her cheek. I wanted to hurt her, at that moment, with a red rage I hadn't felt before.

Jesus, calm down and think.

Why does she look familiar? Where have you seen her before?
She nodded once.

"Over there." She gestured to the corner of the cabin not occupied by the kitchen, the sink, or the cot. There was a gray plastic bucket, like a janitor uses, with a roll of toilet paper looped over a wooden spool.

I'd been hoping for outdoors, of course, but that wasn't going to happen. She wanted me to pee in a bucket in front of her.

"I'm sorry, but I can't." I had pushed myself up to standing, and the room was tilting slightly, although I felt better.

"You can't, huh? You can't?" Unexpectedly, she charged me and I ducked, sending her tripping over the table.

She stood up, out of breath, her yellow frizz sticking to her forehead. She pulled her t-shirt down over her white belly again.

Grabbing my arm, she dragged me to the bucket. "Honey, you will."

· · ·

SESSION #: 2
DATE: JULY 3
TIME: 9:30 A.M.
CATHERINE M. SONDLER, LCSW

Client presented well. Stated she has been "in a better mood" since last session. When asked what changed her mood, she shared, "I saw someone I thought I'd lost."

When questioned further about this "someone," client stated that she was unwilling to talk about the situation at this time. Will pursue this topic at future sessions.

After assessing current level of anxiety and depression symptoms, subject of client's ex-husband was brought up. Client stated that she met her ex-husband at a bar ("even though I don't drink... isn't that funny?") while she was in cosmetology school. Stated relationship progressed quickly and that she experienced pregnancy #3 within a few months. Her mentor, she shared, was extremely worried that client's progress would be derailed by the pregnancy and marriage. "I was just worried I'd lose that baby, too," client stated. Client quickly shifted conversation to her skills as a hairstylist, sharing that she loved her career in cutting and coloring hair. Stated she graduated as one of the best stylists in her class. Demonstrated clear pride at her accomplishment. When redirected to the story of her pregnancy, client's affect flattened. Client looked at her watch and stated she had to leave if she was going to make it to her job on time. When encouraged to remain in the session for five more minutes, she relented, although she was unwilling to discuss her marriage or pregnancy further. She stared blankly into her lap for remaining five minutes. Attempts to engage her were unsuccessful. No homework assigned.

CHAPTER 11

In Raleigh, After

"What were you thinking about once you realized you were trapped in the cabin?"

"I mean, I was scared." Wasn't I stating the obvious? Who in the hell wouldn't be scared?

Catherine nodded. "She'd drugged you, hadn't she?"

"We didn't find out with what until later." At first, I'd been so mad at myself for not fighting back harder; sooner. I'd been beating myself up for not being able to think clearly. Later, I understood better why my thoughts were so muddy. I looked around Catherine's office absently, noticing a small jelly jar filled with yellow flowers. They were pretty. The rest of her office was gray and sterile.

"Do you remember what was going through your mind when you first found yourself in the cabin?"

"I don't know." The truth was, I'd thought of weird things. Memories. She'd kept yanking on my little ponytail while I was there, so I got to thinking about cutting my hair.

"Do you remember when I cut my hair?" I asked, probably seemingly out of the blue.

"I remember when you came to my office with short hair. I don't think you ever told me about cutting it."

"Yeah. Well, it was in the hospital." I paused and took a breath, feeling like the mere memory of the hospital could somehow send me back there. "I'm sure you know this, but there's never a moment—not even when you're in the shower—when you're completely alone there." I'd always felt like I was gasping for breath; drowning. I was suffocating from all those people.

Catherine looked at me. "You wanted to be alone."

I shrugged. I'd sort of understood why the anorexics weren't getting any better. Part of me wanted to be stripped clean, laid bare. I couldn't run but I wanted that feeling of being aerodynamic, free, and insubstantial.

"I wanted to be, I guess, free. Does that make any sense?"

"You wanted to be free of what? People?"

"Yes. I couldn't cope in my usual ways." Hurting myself had become such a means to freedom, and now that it was gone, I wasn't sure how to calm down. I felt too much. I hadn't yet learned where to put those feelings, so sometimes they made their way onto my skin.

"In the hospital, you couldn't cut or burn yourself anymore."

Was I hearing judgment in her voice? I felt hot shame in the center of my chest. I paused.

"You know, I didn't hurt myself to get attention." It hadn't been about wanting to die, either. It was about managing this torrent of emotion that I couldn't control, washing over me from my head to my feet, soaking every cell in my body. Once the rush started, I could only stop it a few ways: running and cutting myself were two of them.

"Very few people who self-injure do it for attention, just as very few do it because they want to die."

Her tone wasn't judgmental, I decided. It sounded neutral. Like always. I was judging myself.

"I just needed to stop feeling so much." One afternoon after I'd been in the hospital for a while, we were in art therapy and were making collages. The project was to take a shoebox and glue pictures from magazines all over the outside that reflected how we thought we looked on the outside. On the inside of the box, we were supposed to cut out words and photos that signified how we felt inside. I still love that shoebox, actually. The inside of my box is completely empty, except for a tiny black star I cut out of a magazine. I never glued anything to the outside.

"Anyway, in the hospital, the counselors let us do this art project with scissors, both because they were watching us like hawks and because the scissors were like the ones pre-schoolers use...dull as hell."

Catherine looked curious and a little afraid. She took a long breath in. Her eyes didn't leave my face. They rarely did.

It had occurred to me like a flash: I needed my outside to get closer to my inside.

"I needed my hair to be gone."

"Your hair?"

"Yeah." I'd gone up to this one aide who was brand new. I knew she couldn't know all the rules yet. Plus, she'd still wanted us to like her. I'd said, "Listen, could you just cut my ponytail off? I'm so sick of it. Cut it as close to the scalp as you can." She'd raised one eyebrow at me. "Cut off your hair? With these? You crazy?" I'd shrugged, like, "Well, I'm in here, aren't I?" And she'd laughed.

"So, she cut my hair off." She'd called another aide in to help the other girls while she unlocked the door to her small office. She'd pulled a good pair of scissors out of her locked desk drawer and asked me one more time if I was sure. I told her my outside didn't match my inside, and she snipped my ponytail off with one long cut. "Congrats," she had said, "now you match."

"With my hair gone, I looked totally different from my former self. I certainly didn't look Cherokee, although people didn't usually peg me as Native American, anyway. They'd ask if I was Mexican, Lebanese…But after the haircut, I looked a lot like how I felt—smaller and sort of, like, untethered."

"Free, maybe?"

"Yeah. I felt free."

CHAPTER 12

On the Blue Ridge

You have to get free.

How the hell was I going to get out? Lorraine had the front door bolted shut and locked. For all I knew, she could have put an alarm on the door. Maybe the place was even booby trapped? I mean, she'd poisoned me.

Even if I could get out of the cabin, I'd still need to find my way back to the van. I had no idea where we were. All those maps I'd studied while I was training suddenly seemed worthless. I was never going to be able to escape, and I had to escape. This woman …what was she going to do to me?

She's crazy. She thinks she's your mother. You're totally screwed.

And then she was sitting on the floor with knitting needles, a half-smile on her face.

"What are you making?" I asked quietly. My head throbbed. My foot throbbed.

"Well, it's going to get cold in a few months," she said. "You can't very well survive the winter in those shorts and that little t-shirt, can you Natalie?" She laughed, and my stomach dropped. Nausea swirled upward like smoke from my belly, to my chest, to my head.

"The winter?"

"Honey, it gets cold up here in the mountains. Not like Raleigh." She snarled, "Raleigh" like it was a filthy word. "It snows a lot. I'm knitting you a cap and some socks."

I felt sweat break out on my upper lip. I didn't want to talk to her. I had to talk to her.

"Thank you," I said, desperate to sound polite. "But what about food? That fridge doesn't look like it can hold much, can it?" I pointed to the mini-fridge in the corner, trying to stuff down my panic.

"Don't you worry about food, honey." She shook her head. "You don't think Mama would let you go hungry, do you? You're not hungry now, are you? Oh, that's right. You said you were. Let's eat something."

She walked over to the kitchenette and pulled two plates from the small shelf above the stove. "Are you still a vegetarian? I've got some beans I can heat up?"

I felt the blood drain from my face.

Jesus Christ. What in the hell is going on?

I swallowed hard. "Um, how'd you...how'd you know I was a vegetarian?"

She smiled, her eyes slits. "What kind of mother would I be if I didn't know that?"

She pulled a can opener from a box on the same shelf and cranked the can open. I wondered what else was in that box—knives?—and decided to check it when I had a spare moment.

How will you ever have a spare moment? She's all over you. How will you ever get away?

I needed to know more about her. I needed to know why I was here.

"How long have you lived in this cabin? Do you like it?" It was a ridiculous question. I couldn't imagine anyone choosing to live there…unless, of course, they'd just abducted a seventeen-year-old distance runner in the middle of the night?

"I haven't been here long, Natalie. Just since Eddie left me." Her face visibly darkened, her brow lowering. "Not that we needed him, anyway, of course."

Who's Eddie?

"But after he left, there was nothing keeping me in Raleigh. No one was using this place, so now it's ours."

"What do you mean, 'no one was using it?'" Did anyone know we were there?

Her eyes landed on me.

"It once belonged to someone who actually cared about me," she said quietly. Then she looked away again.

"Don't you worry about it, missy." She slammed the empty can down on the stovetop. "We are here now, aren't we? We're together. That's what matters."

She slapped an orange plate of baked beans in front of me, then handed me a camping spoon.

"It's no quinoa salad, but it'll do, I hope?" She laughed hysterically as if she'd made the funniest joke ever.

How does she know you're a vegetarian? How does she know you make quinoa salad to bring in your school lunch every day?

"You've drugged me twice," I said, thinking that the risk might be worth it. "Why should I trust you? Why wouldn't you drug me again?"

Lorraine was in my face, one rough hand gripping my chin. "Because I'm telling you to eat, girl," she growled. "You're going to eat." Her voice was low and menacing, no longer the girlish giggle. Sweat collected on her upper lip. She smelled sour.

I took a shaky breath and, freaked out, put the spoon in my right hand. Even with my wrists tied together, which made the process incredibly hard, I started to shovel the beans, lukewarm and too sweet, into my mouth. I was suddenly aware of how hungry I was. The sugar flooded my brain and I began to feel stronger.

"Gosh, you're eating so fast. You must have been hungry, the way you're wolfing that down like a dog." She paused. It was quiet. I listened to the scrape of my spoon on my plate.

"Like Flyer. That dog of yours? He was something."

My stomach iced over. There was a tone in her voice I couldn't quite place. Smugness? She sounded like she was challenging me. She looked me in the eyes.

I put my spoon down.

"My dog? What do you know about my dog?" I asked quietly. Fear settled into my chest.

"Good old Flyer. We knew each other well." There was her maniacal baby laugh again. "That dog sure did like chicken wings. He could put them away like nobody's business."

She lifted her chin and, again, deliberately challenged me with her eyes. I could feel her thoughts: "Go ahead—ask me how I know."

I sat in silence, more terrified by the second. She paused, then looked down at her nails as if casually inspecting them. She looked like she was pretending to be a villain; like she was playing a role.

"That neighborhood where you live. It sure is fancy. I can't imagine living in a place like that." She paused again, sniffing.

Let her talk. Don't say anything until you have to.

"I'd think you'd feel more at home here," she gestured around the cabin, her hands open. "This is who you are. This is who *we* are. No need to get above your raisin'."

She looked like she was about to change the subject again, or clam up, or something. I held my breath, not wanting to say anything that would shut her down.

"You can't just pretend to be from somewhere else, Natalie. You can't just forget."

I took a deep breath. "I'm sorry. I didn't mean to. I didn't know."

She shook her head. "That dog, though. Shame how he had to die. I told him to be a good boy, but he just wouldn't listen."

She smiled at me like we were sharing a joke.

I felt the grip of rage and fear begin to take me, starting in my hands, then moving up my arms into my shoulders and neck. I had to focus on the feeling, had to be mindful of its movement through my body so that I didn't allow the anger to overtake me. I had to be in control.

Take deep breaths, Bright. Remember Catherine's advice: Picture a red stop sign when your feelings start to take over. Showing your emotions now won't help anything.

How did she know about my dog? How did she know anything about me? Who in the hell was she and why had she kidnapped me?

"He sure did love you, though. I mean, that was what got him in the end. I needed to get to you and he got in the way."

As much as I tried to focus on my breathing, to calm myself, the image overtook me in a flash: Flyer lying on his side, peaceful as if he were sleeping, but his eyes open and cold and lifeless. I remembered screaming, trying to pick him up, yelling for Kent, knowing Kent wasn't home from work yet, and then just lying on the floor next to Flyer for hours until Kent came home and found us. He'd scooped me up in his arms, at first sounding angry—"What happened, Bright? What happened?"—and then sounding heartbroken when he realized why I couldn't make a sound. Kent had put me in my bed, fully clothed, and driven Flyer to the vet. He blamed himself, probably still blames himself, for making the mistake of leaving me alone that day. What happened next wasn't his fault, of course. It was my decision. My sadness had been too much; I didn't know how else to cope with it.

Letting those images and feelings overtake me felt frightening and I wasn't sure I'd be able to control myself. I wanted so badly to hurt Lorraine in the same way she had hurt Flyer.

Lorraine laughed again. I took another shaky breath, then a feeling came over me. I can only describe it as God, as intuition, as everyone who'd ever come before me, as love, as whatever light lived inside me, as my connection to everything holy. That feeling shouted, "GO." I had to run. She'd killed my dog trying to get to me. Maybe she'd killed the owners of this cabin, maybe she'd killed more, and I felt sure she'd kill me too if I didn't go. I had to go. It was just a matter of when and how.

I looked around me as stealthily as I could. I needed a hole; an opening. I prayed silently into the void, maybe to God or maybe to my mother: Please. I need a chance to do whatever it takes. I need a miracle.

· · ·

SESSION #: 3
DATE: JULY 11
TIME: 9:30 A.M.
CATHERINE M. SONDLER, LCSW

Client arrived earlier than usual—fifteen minutes prior to appointment time, according to door chime. Presented in good spirits, stating that she had a good week and accomplished a lot. When questioned about accomplishments, client waved her hand and said, "you wouldn't understand." When pressed further, client became angry. Client presented with some manic features, including heightened physical movement, rapid speech, and shallow breathing. When questioned about medication adherence, client insisted that she is continuing to take medications for diagnosed bipolar disorder as prescribed. Denies any negative symptomatology. Denies substance use of any kind. Will continue to monitor and follow up in subsequent sessions.

Client was asked about her previous experiences with therapy. She shared that she found being diagnosed initially helpful as it made her feel "less wrong...and the world looked brighter and cleaner and better." She said therapy improved her relationship with her husband. Took this opportunity to revisit client's marriage and family, topics she had briefly mentioned before shutting down in previous session. She stated that her ex "was a good guy" and that he didn't hit her or the baby or drink much. "He didn't work much either," she said, and affirmed that money was always tight despite her mentor's help. She stated that she and her husband lived in her mentor's guesthouse once her baby was born. When asked if the baby had been born healthy, the client demonstrated loud, inappropriate laughter. She repeated, "hold on loosely...that's what I told myself" three times in a row. When asked what was meant by that statement, the client's affect flattened once more. Client said, "Things were good for a while" before shutting down entirely for the remainder of the session (ten minutes). Expressed concern for the client's mood and mood shifts.

Recommend medication evaluation as soon as possible.

CHAPTER 13

In Raleigh, After

"Weird things have happened to me all my life."

"Weird things?" Catherine had been wearing her "tell-me-more" expression, urging me to go on.

Not just my mom dying, or my dad leaving, or cutting myself. I'm talking about really weird things.

"Like, when I was about 12 I went to the grocery store with Kent." I'd been in the snack aisle picking out some snacks for after school and totally engrossed in it. Kent didn't care what I ate and neither did I, back then. Cheetos and Doritos were my favorites and I didn't really know or care what they might do to my body. I didn't realize that eating better not only made me faster, it made me happier. As I weighed the relative merits of Cool Ranch versus Nacho Cheese, I felt a, like, presence come up behind me. Too close. There was an uncomfortable warmth washing over me, a smell of campfire and peppermint, and anticipation crackling in the air around me. A face leaned toward me and I felt hot breath on my ear.

"This lady walked up to me and whispered, 'They's a root on you.' I turned toward her, scared to death but excited at the same time, and saw the face of this old lady with smooth brown skin and crazy lavender eyes. She was wearing a turban on her head."

"Not your typical supermarket shopper."

I shook my head. Not even close. The lady had come so close to me, but for some reason, I wasn't afraid of her anymore. "You understand me? They's a root on you. Hear me now." She had held both of my shoulders gently, her knotty hands with rings on each finger. I couldn't stop staring into those lavender eyes. I'd never seen anything quite that color, before or since.

"I told her I didn't understand. I didn't know what a 'root' was." The woman had smiled at me, teeth white and eyes purple in her soft brown face. Under her turban, I saw tendrils of white hair escaping. Her dress nearly reached the floor; it was black and too flimsy for the winter weather. She had said, "I seen it in the dirt. You call me. I'm Granny Queen. You call me." She had let go of my shoulders and backed away.

Catherine's eyes widened, and she crossed her legs, listening intently. "I don't know what it is, either."

"She'd said, 'A root. It's a bad spirit. Evil. You got to fight, girl.' And she looked mad. I thought she was mad at me, for some reason." At the time, feeling afraid, I'd nodded like I understood, wondering how I was going to counteract a spell; wondering how it had gotten to me in the first place; wondering what was so wrong with me that a root could find me. "You've just got to learn to fight, girl. You don't learn to fight, all you ever end up doing is running," she'd said.

At that point, I had been kind of ready to be finished with the conversation, but she kept going. "You gotta learn to fight or fightin'll be taught to you. You won't like it that way, neither," she'd said. Then she'd nodded at me and turned on her heel, leaving as suddenly as she'd come.

"What did you make of that? That you needed to fight?"

"At the time? I don't know. I wasn't sure what she'd meant, so I panicked." Panicked was an understatement. I'd chased after her, asking how I was supposed to call her. She had reached into the pocket of her long black dress and pulled out a small piece of paper. She pressed it into my hand. I remember it was warm.

"Call me," she had said while I looked at the paper. Scribbled on it in handwriting I could barely read was a phone number and the name "Granny." As she had turned to walk away from me I saw her fantastic eyes shift to Kent. Unbelievably, as she'd looked at him she'd spit on the ground—right there inside the grocery store—and muttered something under her breath. And then she was gone.

"Did Kent notice you were panicking? Did he see the woman?"

"He just asked me who on earth I'd been talking to. I told him it was Granny Queen."

CHAPTER 14

On the Blue Ridge

I needed to get my strength up. I noted my injuries—my lip was definitely swollen, the side of my face felt bruised, my head was pounding, I had stinging cuts on my face, and my foot was throbbing to the point that it was nearly numb. The fog in my brain seemed to have cleared somewhat, though, so at least I trusted my decision-making powers a bit more. I tried to touch my face and temple, forgetting that my wrists were still tied together and making the gesture way too awkward.

I need to outsmart her. I need to outthink her. I know I can outrun her.

There had never been a time when I had wanted to hurt someone physically, other than myself. I'd never felt my survival depended on my ability to harm someone else, someone who held my safety in her hands. That day was a first. Just thinking about that fact made me nervous. I decided that I wouldn't think about it; that instead, I would just move forward, acting as if all was well; acting as if I had all the time in the world to do all I needed to do. I would just watch and wait.

I thought about my options. She was stronger than she looked. While I'd been drugged, dehydrated, knocked around, and tied up, she was at her peak.

You could confront her.

You could wait until she falls asleep and sneak out.

You could trick her into trusting you.

Tricking her seemed the most attractive, although not necessarily the most plausible, option. Could I get away in time enough to save myself? Could I find my way home?

"Can I ask you a question?" My head was swimming and I was starting to nod off. I didn't know what time it was, but I was suddenly exhausted. I imagined it must be late or early.

"Of course, Natalie." She dropped her knitting needles and smiled at me as if our situation was the most natural thing in the world. "What is it?"

"Why are we here?" I asked her, my face as open as I could make it. I wanted her to respond to the me she loved, the Natalie she imagined, rather than this real, dirty, disobedient Bright.

"We are here because we've come home, honey," she responded.

"Where were we before, though?"

"We were apart from one another. They had you. They were keeping me from you and I had to, you know, take drastic measures."

I smiled at her, pulling up all my reserves and forcing myself to imagine she was my actual mother. It took everything I had; everything inside me.

"So, where were you before?"

"Well, at first I was still with Eddie. We were in the trailer, where you lived with us." She looked me in the eye and winked as if I might somehow know what she was talking about.

"You remember how nice I made your room, don't you Natalie? I bought you that princess bed even though I had to take on extra shifts to pay for it. I bought it for you."

She sighed, the smile draining from her face. "It broke my heart when I had to watch it burn."

At the word "burn," my exhausted ears perked up and I sat up straighter in my chair.

Focus, Bright. Stay here.

"Why did you have to watch it burn?" I asked quietly, afraid to hear the answer. I wondered if this was how Catherine felt when she asked me questions she really didn't want the answers to.

She laughed in her high-pitched, near-hysterical way.

"Well, what was I going to do? Let him tell those lies about me, honey?" She laughed so hard that she doubled herself over and threw her knitting down on the floor.

"I burned it all down. I burned him down." She was laughing so hard she could barely speak. Her eyes closed as she threw her head back and laughed for a long, horrifying minute.

Finally, she gathered up her knitting again, straightening the yarn as she did so. When she looked at me again, her face was serene. She wiped tears from her eyes, pulling at the loose skin there as she did so.

"I needed to keep you safe and with me, Natalie." She nodded toward my covered arms. "I'm just sorry you got hurt in the fire, is all. I never meant to hurt you. You weren't supposed to be there."

I took a deep breath. I wished I could understand her delusion. I had burn scars, but I also had the psychiatry bills to prove she hadn't given them to me.

"I wasn't ...I just ...I need to know what you want. What do you want from me? What do you want from me now?" My voice sounded hollow, growing louder with each question. It was unrecognizable.

Before I could turn my face toward her, I fell to the ground. She'd punched me in the head. It didn't even hurt, at first, but then I was afraid I'd black out. I couldn't feel the tips of my toes and my head was floating.

Stay here. Stay here.

"What the hell?" I screamed at her, tasting blood.

"Jesus! Why did you hit me?" I breathed in ragged gasps. There was dark around the edges of my vision.

I pulled my legs underneath me, aware of the pain in my foot, aware of my stench, aware of the rough planks under my hands.

She laughed. It was a tinkling sound, like a fairytale princess. Incongruous with the animal snarl on her face, still blurry and dark around the edges of my sight. Her face looked like an oiled potato, plump and creased around the eyes and lips. Her black eyes glowed.

How do you know her?

"Respect, Natalie, R-E-S-P-E-C-T," she sang, trilling like a sparrow. "When you treat others with respect, you receive it in return."

She smiled, then suddenly delivered a kick so swift and powerful to the side of my bent knee that I screamed out, "No!"

When I'd fallen, I must have cut my forehead, and I felt a drop of blood skating toward my eye.

"And that was for your nasty language."

Think, Bright.

"Mama," I said quickly, softly, the word carving a painful rut through my dry lips, "Mama, I'm sorry." I squeezed my eyes shut.

Think.

"I need a doctor." I looked up at her, doing my best imitation of an apologetic daughter, hoping the blood had made an obvious trail down my face, painting a sympathetic picture.

Her lips snaked upward on her plump face and she raised her eyebrows.

"Oh, honey. Know what's better than a doctor?" She reached into her giant patchwork purse, shuffling around receipts and candy wrappers and brochures. At last, she pulled out a large white case with a red cross on it and set it on the floor.

"A mama."

She turned her back to me, crouching down as she opened the first aid kit, and I didn't think. For a moment, time stood still. The air stilled. Was this my miracle? There was a low buzzing of energy in the room as a voice whispered in my ear:

Do it. Do it now.

I reached over to the pot of baked beans. I gripped the handle in both hands, noticing for a millisecond how the sheer pink nail polish I'd been so proud of hours ago had chipped off the nails of my thumbs and middle fingers. And then, with every ounce of strength I had, I cracked the pot over the back of her skull.

Once. Twice. Three times.

A guttural cry escaped my mouth without me intending it. The sound of the pot hitting her skull cut through the quiet—a sickening metallic thud.

I wasn't myself. It was as if someone, something, else had taken over my body for those moments. I felt like I was floating above my body and watching myself, unsure of how I'd gotten there in the first place.

Baked beans rained all over the floor and all over her back; they splashed on my legs. Lorraine was face down on the cabin floor, her yellow hair dark with the beans. I leaped over her still figure, one shoe sliding on a spill of beans, legs fueled by adrenaline. I didn't look back. I didn't even glance at her. My wrists still tied tight together, I grabbed at the deadbolt attached to the metal band across the front door. My hands were slick with sweat and I couldn't get a good grip. I thought I heard movement behind me; rustling. Was she getting up?

Again, I tried to twist the deadbolt, and my shaking hands slipped off.

It's now or never. Do it. This may be your only chance.

Finally, I gritted my teeth and, both hands holding on for dear life, turned the lock. With a solid and infinite click, I twisted the doorknob, and I was out. Out into the boundless darkness, no breath in my body, no light in my eyes. Fresh, wide night all around.

Run.

I had no idea which way to go. Silently screaming, no noise escaping me, I just ran, keeping my eyes on the sky at first to follow the scant light of the stars.

I took a deep breath, then I whispered, not sure to whom, in a hoarse voice:

"Show me which way to go," I was shivering from exhaustion and overwhelmed by the sky. The moon was bright. "Shine in the right direction."

I moved forward along the tree-lined driveway of the cabin, looking up at the sky. All the night hikes I'd been on at camp, all of the early morning runs I'd spent studying the constellations, all of it came back to me. I saw Lyra, The Lyre, and I thought of the seven sisters, the ancient constellation guiding women to safety, holding them in their grasp. I didn't know how I'd do this, but I had to start.

It was dark, but I had the moon and the stars. I thought of the headlamp I'd grudgingly worn when I was stolen—it must've ended up in Lorraine's car somewhere—and wished I'd had it. Any extra light would've saved me from twisting my ankle on a rock or going down in a ditch.

Slowly, I ran with my arms extended straight in front of me—a horror-movie zombie. A few times, the tips of my fingers met tree branches. With my wrists tied together, my balance felt especially off.

Look at the sky. Let your eyes adjust. The stars know you.

CHAPTER 15

In Raleigh, Before

"You mentioned earlier that one of your nicknames had been 'Garbage Girl'? Tell me about that." I knew Catherine would ask about it sooner or later. She didn't miss a thing. Sometimes she'd even sit on something I'd said for a week or two, only bringing it back up when I'd nearly forgotten it.

I sighed. "Some kids at school called me Garbage Girl for a while." They had meant it as an insult, of course, but I didn't really take it that way until later. All I knew was that they told us in school that littering was wrong. I also knew that when I saw garbage on the floor, on the ground, on the sidewalk, I had the ability to pick it up and put it in the recycling bin or the trash can.

This made sense to me. What didn't make sense to me was the act of walking over things; of ignoring what you didn't want to see and just stepping right by. I couldn't believe that everyone didn't just pick up trash and throw it away. I remember walking to school behind Mackenzie Zapata one morning.

I saw her throw an empty soda bottle on the sidewalk. I'd been so angry I could barely control myself.

I laughed a little. "This girl dropped a bottle on the way to school and I screamed at her for it. I shoved the trash in her face," I remember her eyes looked like moons and I noticed freckles dotting her nose. I asked her why she wouldn't just pick up the bottle. I asked her whose responsibility she thought it was to clean up the earth.

She ran away from me, but I was faster. I sprinted past her and dropped the bottle in the recycling bin on the edge of campus.

"By the time Mackenzie got to school that day, of course, I was Garbage Girl."

Later, the story had morphed into something unrecognizable. According to the playground gossip, I'd actually smacked Mackenzie over the head with the soda bottle. I'd then licked the edge of it, for good measure. The next day, the story was that my house was full of garbage. My room was a mountain of garbage. My stepdad and I went out late at night together and picked through dumpsters in search of furnishings for our home, clothes, and food for our next meal. I was a dumpster diver, a derelict. I was Garbage Girl.

Looking back, I see the humor in this. It still stings, though, when I imagine the earnest and sweet-faced girl I had been, wanting nothing more than to save the planet and instead being ridiculed for doing the right thing. I'm sad for that girl. I'm sad for the other kids in my class who likely stepped over trash from that point on, for fear of earning my title. My embarrassment and mortification led to more undoing, not less.

"What happened after that?"

"I guess, I don't know, I became Garbage Girl."

In fact, I'd started doing something really strange, without even realizing I was doing it. I'd run in the dark before school (this part wasn't strange—I'd always avoided running when other people could see me) and I'd pick up garbage along the way and throw it into the park's garbage cans. Then, one day, I'd lost track of time and had to get home to get ready for school, so I brought the garbage with me and shoved it in my closet. I showered and dressed in a hurry; being tardy meant having to get a pass at the front office from the assistant principal. When I arrived home from school that afternoon, I saw the small pile of chip bags and soda cans, and I didn't put it in the garbage or recycling. Why I didn't, I wasn't sure…but I didn't. The next morning, I did the same thing: I ran, picked up trash, came home, and put it in my closet. Maybe a part of me was thinking, "You call me Garbage Girl? I'll show you Garbage Girl!"

"I mean, would you call hoarding garbage in my closet a compulsive behavior? To the point that, after a couple of weeks of collecting, I didn't have room in my closet for anything else?"

Catherine just looked at me without answering. She did that sometimes. After a few minutes, she asked, "Did it feel compulsive to you?"

"I don't know. It's not like I even had some master plan for all that trash, at first. I just went into Kent's office when he was still at work, got a piece of cardboard and some super glue, and started piling it on. A can here, a wad of paper there...I glued it all together into one giant tower. Then, I set it on my desk and forgot about it."

As the memories came back to me, they felt harder and harder to talk about with Catherine. She just kept looking at me, though, expecting me to go on.

"For the next couple of days, every time I went into my room I would stare at the trash sculpture. I liked how solid it was; how its shape resembled a pine tree or a medieval tower."

I remembered that it had needed something, though. One night when Kent had gone to sleep early, I wandered out into our dusty garage, overgrown with little boxes of nails, cleaning supplies we'd never used, ant killer, and paint. On a high shelf, I saw a can of black spray paint. I climbed up and grabbed it.

Once I'd sprayed the garbage it looked perfect. I'd taken it on the back deck to do it and had managed to only get a small smudge or two of black on the wood. Not that Kent would have noticed or that it would have mattered—we didn't exactly keep a perfect house. But my artwork? It was beautiful in a way I couldn't even describe. I knew I'd found something else that could help me.

"I started copying my favorite constellations from the internet: Ursa Minor, Hydra, Aquarius, Canis Major,

Cassiopeia, Orion…Then, I used my sketches of the constellations to make them out of the trash."

What I didn't tell Catherine was that I'd painstakingly built the constellations to scale with string and white thumbtacks. Once I got them right, I removed these and painted white dots of varying sizes where the stars should be. I mean, I spent hours doing this. Looking back, I wonder what Kent thought I was doing for all that time alone in my room. I wonder if Kent even noticed.

"In two weeks, my room had become overrun with black and white constellation garbage sculptures."

Catherine's face was unreadable, but I could imagine what she was thinking: *She's even more screwed up than I thought.*

Sure, it was weird. But when I walked into my room each afternoon it took my breath away: it was like a landscape of heaven. It was like the photos I'd seen of the West Texas sky; peaks and valleys of old trash made new, made gorgeous. I could even imagine the Aurora Borealis, pink and green, spilling through my room. It overwhelmed me. It changed my mood. It made coming home okay.

Until it didn't.

Until the day I came home from school, a particularly bad day when not only Mackenzie but everyone else in gym class had made fun of me; a day when, at lunch, everyone pegged me with empty candy wrappers and water bottles and soda cans when the lunch monitor's back was turned and then, when her fat angry face finally turned back around, conspired and pointed at me: "Bright's throwing things, ma'am!" After school detention for me, not that I minded being away from home. It was a bad day, though, all around.

When I finally walked home after detention, unlocked the front door, greeted Flyer, and escaped to my room, I was exhausted. I thought I might try to make another piece, or maybe just admire what I'd already created. I opened the door to my room and gasped.

"But, one day I came home and Kent had thrown them all away."

My room was as blank as toast. Not a dark sky sculpture anywhere. Not a piece of trash in the closet. Nothing. Just my prison cell.

I tore out of the room screaming for Kent, who—of course—was still at work. I picked up the phone and he'd barely answered when I started yelling.

"Why'd you do it, Kent? Where is my art? Why'd you throw it away?" I had hated the sound of my voice, the tears dribbling onto the old phone's receiver.

"What? Bright? Are you okay?" He had sounded like he'd been deep in thought; solving some complex engineering problem or whatever the hell else he did all day.

"No, goddamn it! I'm not okay!" I had shouted. "Where are my sculptures?"

"Brighty!' He'd scolded. "If you're talking about the garbage that was in your room, I put it out in the garbage cans where it belongs—"

I couldn't let him finish his sentence because I had needed to sprint to the curb. I didn't even hang up the phone. Had the trash truck come yet? I ran out and ripped the lid off the can, bending over at the waist and tilting the can toward me.

Empty. I'd started to cry, sinking back on my butt in the street, putting my head in my dirty hands.

Then, unbelievably, I'd heard snickers.

I had looked up to see Tommy Shannon and Marco Ortiz on their bikes in front of my house.

"Oh, what's wrong?" the bucktoothed Tommy had said. "Run outta trash, Garbage Girl? Don't cry about it!" He picked up a stray napkin from the curb and tossed it in my direction.

"Freak!" Fat Marco had yelled. And then they were gone.

Finally, Catherine spoke. "That must have been so hard for you. All that work gone in a moment."

"It was a bad day. Another bad day."

. . .

Finn, N.C.—Baxter County deputies and search and rescue crews are currently looking for a 17-year-old girl who went missing from the route of a local ultra-relay race at around 11:30 p.m. Saturday night.

Cole Martinez of the Baxter County Sheriff's Office said Bright Shelby of Raleigh was a member of a six-person relay team running the North Carolina Mountain Relay. The race, in its 7th year, attracts a small but elite group of distance runners, says race director Jimmy Holden. "We are confident that the sheriff's team will locate Bright as soon as possible." Holden, longtime race director, says the relay's course has many difficult stretches. "This is a complicated event. People get sick on the trail, people get lost. No one has ever remained lost for any period of time, and Bright Shelby won't be the first."

Miss Shelby's first 14-mile run began just south of Rocky Knob Bike Park. Her teammates reported her missing Saturday night after she failed to meet her team's van at the scheduled check point located near U.S. 345 South.

Bright is an experienced distance runner accustomed to rough trail terrain, but unfamiliar with the Blue Ridge. She is described as 5'8" and approximately 115 pounds, with dark hair and olive skin. She was last seen wearing a long-sleeved white running shirt, black running shorts, and red running shoes when she went missing. Her stepfather says she has identifying burn scars over much of both forearms. Please contact the Baxter County Sheriff's Department at (828) 733-3000 with any information.

CHAPTER 16

On the Blue Ridge

I took a deep breath and ran, moderately at first, then picking up speed as I noticed that I was running on something that felt like a trail. I tried to feel it with my feet and to let the stars guide me. I sped up, the sky brightening by a few degrees. I didn't feel tired. I didn't feel hungry or sick. My foot didn't hurt at all.

You are free.

And with every step I took, I felt the miles spreading like blood between Lorraine and me. But I didn't want to think about her yet. I only wanted to think about my feet pounding along the path and the constellations above me. When I focused on the seven sisters, I stopped hearing the metallic thwack of the pot on the back of Lorraine's skull. The pot I'd hit her with, more than once. How many times had I hit her?

You did what you had to do to get out of there. You are alive.

The soles of my running shoes were already muddy and clogged with the leaves they'd picked up along the trail. The adrenaline that had been fueling me started to disappear, and my legs felt heavier. It was disorienting, this experience of running without any visible destination. In an instant, I noticed lights in the distance. Was I nearing a town? I was thrilled and terrified all at the same time.

Help could be ahead. So could Lorraine.

Arms extended, I ran on. The light I saw grew larger in relation to how small I felt. I could still run, at least. Thank you, God.

I kept going. I didn't hear any other cars or people ahead, but I had faith: where there was light, there had to be people. I noticed my throbbing head and foot only when I slowed down, so I kept running fast. Never mind that I didn't know where I was running to. In the darkness, I wasn't self-conscious of the fact that I was running with my arms straight out in front of me, my wrists still tied together. I was a part of the night. I was a part of the scenery. I was invisible.

Then, like an animal, I smelled life. Leaves burning, cooking smells. Fire. I knew there must be life nearby if I smelled it. I didn't slow my pace, though, letting the lights and the smells guide me forward.

And there it was: a road. Which road didn't really matter, and there weren't exactly street signs guiding drivers through those mountain passes in the Blue Ridge. I felt stronger again, even if it was only adrenaline driving me...adrenaline that would die out soon enough. I couldn't think about the fact that I'd need water and food and rest.

Keep running. Keep moving. Push forward.

For the first time, I realized my GPS watch was missing. Of course Lorraine had taken it, but this felt disorienting nonetheless. I just wanted to know what time it was, but it felt like the sun would be up soon. The sun was my best friend and my worst enemy. I needed to run as close to civilization as I could before the sun rose. I had to create as much distance as possible between Lorraine and me. Now.

CHAPTER 17

In Raleigh, After

"So, did you ever end up calling Granny Queen?" Catherine asked.

"Yeah. I called her the same day. I'm not sure I want to talk about this now."

Talking to Catherine about Granny Queen, just remembering Granny Queen, gave me a pit in my stomach. It brought everything back. When I'd called Granny's number later that night, after Kent assumed I was safely asleep and I'd waved my goodnights, she'd repeated that there was a root on me. I had looked up "root" online because I'd never heard of a root until that day. Granny had seen it in the dirt, she'd said, that someone had cursed me and I needed to do something about it.

The internet said root medicine had started in Africa and the Caribbean. Some people might call it witchcraft or voodoo, but in some ways, believing that someone had cursed me was easier than thinking that God just had it in for me. I'm part Cherokee Indian, even if my dad never really claimed me. My native tradition believed in symbols, mystery, roots, in what some people might consider witchcraft. And how different were my mother's rosary beads from a root doctor's shrine, anyway?

"What happened when you called?" Catherine wasn't going to let me off the hook, clearly.

"It was like she was just waiting for me. She answered right away."

Granny's voice on the phone had been thin but confident.

"Yes, child. I know it's you," she'd said as I awkwardly tried to identify myself. "You've got a root on you. I know you can't come out to see me, child, but I'm on' tell you what to do."

She had seemed able to anticipate my words before I said them. Was it possible that she really was a magical root doctor, able to fix what was wrong with me? Could someone have really put a spell on me to begin with? If so, why?

She'd said, "Here's what you're on' do. Go out to that field behind your house, now. You pick you some dandelions, just two. Pull off all them little flyaway leaves. Stick the leaves in a burlap bag. Gotta be burlap, now. No plastic. Then get up to that graveyard down the road and dig you up some dirt. Put it in the little burlap bag, and you tie that bag 'round your neck with a red yarn."

This had freaked me out. Did she really know where I lived, and that a field of dandelions grew right behind my house? Did she know about the graveyard less than a mile from the entrance to my neighborhood? Or did everyone have dandelions behind their houses and graveyards "down the road"?

"And then," she had said, "find you a dime—a shiny one. Stick it in your right sock right near your ankle bone. You gonna do this today, child. You call me if you need more." She had paused for a few seconds. "You got the light in you, child. Do this for the light in you."

"When I talked to Granny on the phone," I told Catherine, staring at my hands in my lap, "I felt hopeful, I guess."

And like that, Granny hung up the phone. My conversation with her had felt like a dream. I mean, had she said a dime? Around my right ankle? I remember scribbling her instructions on the back of my math binder and wanting so much for these things to change me. Feeling in my heart that Granny somehow knew me and, most importantly, knew how to fix me. I went to sleep that night vowing that the next day, I would go out to the dandelion field and the graveyard. The next day, I would buy some red string and some ribbon and I would find a shiny new dime. She'd seen light in me! When I woke up in the morning, the first voice I heard was the one in my head:

Idiot. Do you really think a dime and a bag of dirt can change your life? Do you really think that crazy old lady has any idea what she's talking about? If you do, you're even crazier than she is.

I did my best to ignore the voice all morning. I distracted myself by daydreaming about how my life might be different, how I might be different, if I followed Granny Queen's instructions. I was even able to ignore the boys who threw rocks at my ankles on the walk to school because I had a plan. Things were going to change because I was going to change, and I allowed excitement to well up inside me all morning.

It was Math class, fifth period, before things started to fall apart. First, I heard snickering to my right as I was watching our teacher work out problems on the white board. When I turned to see what the laughter was all about, I realized the girls—MJ and Carly—had taken my binder and were reading the notes I'd taken while on the phone with Granny Queen the night before.

"I mean, 'red string around neck'?" MJ giggled.

"'Graveyard'? 'Burlap bag'?" Carly stopped laughing and sneered at me. "God, you're a freak, Bright," she stage-whispered. "I mean, maybe you're more than that. Maybe this isn't funny at all." She paused. "Whose neck are you tying string around? Are you, like, some kind of devil worshiper?" Her bubble-gum pink lips drew back in mock horror, and she and MJ laughed so loudly that the teacher turned away from the board for a moment and shushed them. When I looked down at my desk, my face hot with shame, I saw that one of the girls had returned my math notebook. She'd scrawled over my notes in red marker, "BRIGHT SHELBY LOVES SATAN." I could feel the rest of the class staring at me; could hear the murmurs throughout the room. I ripped off the back cover of my notebook and tore it in half, throwing it in the garbage can on my way out of class.

"That sounds positive," Catherine said neutrally. "Feeling hopeful."

I cut my arms deeper than usual that day, and I had a hard time stopping the bleeding.

"Like everything else," I said, "it didn't last."

I never did go to the dandelions, either.

CHAPTER 18

On the Blue Ridge

I hadn't yet passed a single car on that mountain road; not a single house. I ran past nothing but land behind fences and wide, blue-tinged darkness. The pine trees rose up like guardians. I felt safe in a way, protected by the dark and the pines until I let myself remember. Then my breaths started coming in rasps. I had to focus in order to control my breathing. The thought that Lorraine might already be hunting me kept me running, surrounded by the beauty of the Blue Ridge.

Kent would love this place.

I was suddenly struck with affection for Kent. I usually did my best to keep Kent out of my world, telling myself it was for his own protection. He'd already been through so much—my mother's cancer and death, then what I'd put him through—that I hated the thought of weighing him down with more.

I remembered his face when he came to visit me at the hospital for the first time. He was so confused; so burdened with grief. Looking at his face that day just made me want to disappear.

"Just tell me why, Brighty," there were thick purple pouches under his eyes, wet with tears, and I'd had to turn my face away from all the pain I'd caused him. I stared down at my bandaged arms, at the scratchy hospital sheets, at my ragged cuticles. Anything to avoid his face.

I'd just shaken my head. There was no "why." How could I explain who I was: the kind of person who couldn't tolerate living in her own skin? The kind of person so disgusted with herself that she had to watch herself bleed, watch herself burn? How could I explain this to someone who loved me, probably because he couldn't see who I was on the inside?

The truth, of course, was that I didn't really understand why I did it. I tried not to think about it, but those moments crept up on me when I least expected them, when I was most alone, like running through darkness. I couldn't outrun my thoughts. I hadn't yet, anyway. In the Blue Ridge Mountains, with no one to rely on but myself, I had to consider all the choices I'd made; even the ones that didn't feel like choices.

· · ·

It was early morning, the light tinged with blue. I felt like I'd probably run about six miles, and I hadn't come across another human being. There was a small herd of goats on the side of the road, but I saw no house, no farm to which they belonged. I decided to keep going, banking on the fact that more distance was better than less. The road was narrow and craggy, and I had to watch my step constantly to keep from twisting my ankle.

Then, headlights shone behind me.

Hide.

I glanced to the road's shoulder, looking for brush to hide in. It was too late. The vehicle barreled around me—it must've seen me—and then slowed down.

Shit.

It was a pick-up truck, so it wasn't Lorraine. Relief washed over me like water, raising goosebumps on my arms and legs. The beat-up truck stopped a few yards in front of me, its lights beacons. I sped up to the passenger side of the truck.

Don't be afraid.

I saw the driver bend over to the passenger side and manually roll down the window. I breathed in sharply and looked inside the truck.

"Girl, what are you doing out here?" The man's face was friendly. He had a thick blond mustache and wore a dirty Appalachian State cap on his long hair, but his eyes were kind. "You realize it's the goddamn middle of the night?" He laughed to himself. He looked to be maybe in his twenties or early thirties and spoke with a thick North Carolina accent.

"You need a ride? Where you headed?" He went on, not waiting for an answer. He looked me up and down, and I was suddenly aware of the fact that I hadn't seen myself in a mirror since leaving the van the night before. My wrists were still bound together, a fact he noticed but didn't immediately mention. I must've been covered in blood, sweat, mud—I must've looked like I'd been through hell.

It's over now, though. Your hell is over.

I laughed a little along with him. I felt hysteria welling up in my chest as I understood that I was about to be rescued.

You're safe now. Just relax.

"I was running the ultra-relay. You know, the relay race? This lady told me there was a bear on the loose and I needed to get into her car. She was lying. She kidnapped me. I had to escape." I raised my bound wrists in front of my face to illustrate my point, realizing how crazy I sounded.

The man's smile started to fade a little, relaxing his wide blond mustache into a bushy arc, and he looked me up and down again.

"Hmm." He nodded his head again, the bill of his cap dipping, looking concerned. He shifted in his seat, pulling a pocket knife out of his belt. I must've flinched because he raised his palms in surrender, the knife in his left hand.

"For your wrists. You can do it yourself if you want." I shook my head and he sliced the ropes cleanly. It was a sharp knife, I noticed.

"Get on in the truck, now." He opened the passenger door. "We'll get you where you need to go. Won't we, Kenny?"

I stepped up into the cab of the truck as I noticed a man in the backseat. His hair was black and greasy, covered by a stocking cap. In the interior light of the truck, his eyes were narrow and red-rimmed, and he had a black tattoo snaking up the side of his neck. The truck smelled like smoke and something chemical. It was hot.

The relief that had washed over me just moments before evaporated in the heat of the front seat. I had a bad feeling about this. I clenched my hands into fists and weighed my options for a split second.

Help. Or Lorraine. Or something else.

I took another deep breath, tasting that chemical smell in the back of my throat. Was it coming from the truck's engine? Was it drugs? I'd never really been around drugs, but it was always all over the news how meth and opioids were such big problems in the mountains. I'd made my decision, though—I'd chosen the possibility of help. What else could I choose?

Buckling my seatbelt, I slammed the door.

"I'm Lawrence and this here's Kenny," the driver said, gesturing to the back of the truck. "What's your name?"

"Bright," I said it with as much strength as I could muster, already feeling too vulnerable with the red-eyed Kenny sitting right behind me.

"Bright, huh? Well, that's a crazy-ass name for a crazy-ass story, ain't it?" A gravelly voice came from the back seat, accompanied by breath that smelled like liquor. "And what the hell happened to you?"

I addressed Lawrence, who lit a cigarette with one hand and steered with the other. He nodded at the cigarette, offering me one with his eyes. I shook my head. In the orange glow of the lighter, I saw deep lines around his mouth.

"I don't know. My dad was Cherokee." I said, realizing too late that I didn't owe them any kind of an explanation. "Can you take me to the police station?"

Kenny lay a hand on the back of my neck and it felt like an electric shock; I jumped three inches off my seat. My shoulders, which had been trembling slightly, were now shaking violently from fear.

"Easy there, Pocahontas," he drawled, "take the edge off now." He passed me a bottle in a brown paper bag; it looked like whiskey. I shook my head.

"Take the edge off." He repeated, his voice streaked with menace this time, and I noticed Lawrence looking at me out of the corner of his eye. "This'll calm you down."

"Come on, now, Kenny, if the girl don't want a drink—"

"Shut up and drive, asshole." The hair on the back of my neck stood up and Lawrence nodded to me, almost imperceptibly. He let the truck idle for another moment as he reached behind him and handed me a dark hoodie. I didn't refuse it, as much as a part of me wanted to. I was suddenly and inexplicably cold enough to zip it up to my chin. The truck started moving forward.

Jesus Christ, Bright, just play along.

I lifted the bottle to my lips and pretended to swallow.

"There you go," Kenny slurred, and I felt his disgusting hand on my neck, "That's a good girl."

"I really need water. Do you have any?" Lawrence handed me a plastic water bottle—the same brand as the bottle Lorraine had given me—and I drank half of it in one gulp.

I heard Kenny shift in his seat; unbuckle his seat belt.

"I got lots of room back here, pretty girl," he murmured, "why on'tcha come on back here and keep me company?"

I noticed Lawrence sitting up straighter at the wheel.

"Aw man, leave the girl alone." And as soon as Lawrence finished his sentence, a wild fist flew out of the back seat and landed on the side of his head. Lawrence cursed, trying to right the truck and regain control of the wheel at the same time. In a flash of lights and a bump of tires, the truck bounded off the road and onto the shoulder where it broke through a fence, sliding to a stop on the grass of someone's farm. The sun peeked orange from the earth's edge. I was frozen in my seat, shaking, the side of my head throbbing where it had smacked the window.

"Go! Get out of here! Go!" Lawrence's face was in mine, chanting at me, his eyes wild, his breath hot. "Just go. I'll call the cops, I promise. Run!"

I didn't think. I didn't do anything but grab the door handle and pull. The door was halfway open when I felt a cold hand on my shoulder. Kenny sat up in the back seat. He'd hit his head on something. Blood seeped from below his stocking cap.

"Get over here! You little bitch!" His yellow teeth were bared like a dog's as I jumped out of the pick-up truck and sprinted as fast as my legs could move. Behind me, I heard rustling; scuffling. I heard what sounded like Lawrence blocking Kenny.

"Just sleep it off. Just let the girl be, Kenny." More shuffling.

My mind wasn't working, but—thank God—my legs were. I could barely feel the soles of my feet as I ran blindly through the semi-darkness.

Can't slow down. Can't stop. Keep breathing.

My heart was pounding faster than my feet. It was too dark to see exactly where I was, but too light to hide. How long had we been in the car? How far had we driven? Which direction was I running?

Come on, sun. Rise. Show me the way.

. . .

SESSION #: 4
DATE: JULY 18
TIME: 9:30 A.M.
CATHERINE M. SONDLER, LCSW

Client arrived early to session again. This time, according to door chime, arrival was 20 minutes prior to appointment time.

Asked why she had arrived early, and client responded that she just wanted to be on time. Didn't press further. Instead, asked client to pick up where she had left off during the previous session when she said things had been good for a while with her baby. Client took a deep breath. She shared that her baby was two and a half and the baby's father was watching her while she was working. Client said her husband fell asleep in front of the TV and her toddler went out to play in the front yard. She stated that she received a call at work that her toddler had run into the street to retrieve a ball and that a lumber truck had come around the corner and hit her. Client stated that when her husband called her at work to tell her, "I knew right away she was dead." Stated she didn't believe she deserved the life she'd had, and it only made sense that it had been taken from her. When asked why she believed this, client did not respond. Client appeared dissociative while sharing the story. She stated she had to stay in the hospital for some time following her child's death for psychiatric treatment. "I never got over it," she said, "but I learned to live around it." When asked how she was able to manage, client shared that she had good support from her therapist, from friends, and from her husband. In the middle of sharing about her support system, client made eye contact and stated she had to leave early. Client left the session with 15 minutes remaining, despite efforts to get her to stay.

CHAPTER 19

In Raleigh, Before

"You probably want to know why I started hurting myself."

Catherine looked at me, eyebrows raised.

I knew I'd have to tell her eventually. Now was as good a time as any. In the hospital, once I was well enough to talk, that was all anybody ever wanted to know. The what-would-make-you-do-this question flooded me day and night; in individual sessions with the night shift therapists, in group treatment led by the counseling interns who looked so damn scared of us all I thought they might burst into tears at any moment, and even the moment I walked into the director's office, the guy who'd been there for 22 years and seen it all, all anyone wanted to know was why.

"Do you want to tell me? Do you know why?"

Jesus, I thought anyone who had ever watched an ABC Family special on cutting would know the answer to that or at least have a decent guess. Cutting, self-mutilation, whatever you want to call it. Parents and teachers and therapists were obsessed with the topic, there for a while anyway, which is actually how I got the idea to do it for the first time. The day I found out my mother had died, I just ran and ran and ran. The medicine for the pain was a different kind of pain.

"I over-treated my symptoms, I guess."

"Over-treated your symptoms?"

Sometimes running was enough medicine, the pain of overtraining was enough, but other times I needed to cut. The day my mother died, the day I ran across the park and down to the lake, over and over again, up and down hills, till I was sweaty and exhausted and could barely move another muscle, I tripped on a tree root in front of the school and totally wiped out. I mean, I just ate shit right there in front of the school. Luckily, I'd put my hands out to break my fall, but my palms were bloodied and both knees of my jeans were torn through. I looked around to see if anyone had seen me fall (no one had) and I stared down at the dirty, bloodied palms of my hands. They were stinging like crazy. Both knees were killing me and the pain actually brought tears to my eyes. But I wasn't thinking about my mother.

"I realized that hurting kept me from thinking. Or maybe from feeling."

Catherine nodded.

Hurting myself was a secret I carried with me for a few months. Like, literally. I put a rock in my shoe in the mornings, before school, and I'd keep it there all day long. I'd always pick a jagged one, one that would poke into my toe just so and usually, hopefully, make me bleed. During the day, if I ever felt like crying, I'd press down as hard as I could on that rock, hard enough to make it pierce the skin, and it kept the tears in.

"So, you found a way to keep your emotions together. You found an outlet."

"I guess."

Then when I was in fifth grade, our teacher, Mrs. Labruzzo, made us watch a video on cutting one Friday. I'm now pretty sure that Mrs. Labruzzo made us watch videos on Fridays because she was too hungover to deal with teaching, but back then I had no idea. By then, I'd graduated to putting a piece of broken glass—usually just something I'd found walking to school, during my garbage collecting, in my pocket and jamming it into my thigh if or when I needed to. This video old drunk Mrs. Labruzzo showed us, though, talked about girls who cut themselves with razor blades and burned themselves with cigarettes. They did it to escape from emotional pain, and though the video was meant to warn us, I was fascinated. More than fascinated, I was *fixed*. So I thought, anyway.

"You coped. You found a way."

I nodded. And so it started, for real. The secret-keeping. The blood-letting. The burning. But also, the final and truly unbelievable relief I couldn't get anywhere else—not from running, not from alcohol, not from sleep. Yeah, I tried drinking a few times. Once when I was 13 and Kent left me at home for a rare night out with his buddies from before mom and me, I dug into the way-back of the pantry and found a dusty bottle of what I now think was Scotch. I was savvy enough, from TV and movies, to know you weren't supposed to just drink liquor straight, so I mixed it with some Seven Up in a big plastic cup and drank the whole thing in two sips. Ten seconds after it was down, it was back up again. I never felt anything but sick. I tried again, once, when I was a little older. This girl Martina had invited me to a sleepover at her house (she was new to school and apparently hadn't gotten the memo that I wasn't to be invited to anything…ever) and one of the girls, a blond-haired tennis player who ended up moving to Washington or Wisconsin, had brought a bottle of peach schnapps rolled in her sleeping bag. She passed it around and each of us drank some. After about three rounds, Martina started crying and told us all about how her uncle had tried to make out with her when she was little. I stopped drinking. Martina ended up throwing up in the toilet all night and her mother drove me and the blonde girl home at midnight.

I paused. "Most of the therapists I've worked with assumed I was sexually abused."

"Were you?"

I shook my head. "Just generally messed up, I guess."

"So, you said you never tried drugs?"

I shook my head. Drugs were never something I was interested in. I was terrified by the episodes of *Intervention* I watched late at night after Kent went to bed. I think a part of me could imagine slipping into that oblivion too easily. But leave it to *Intervention* to *not* scare me straight when all was said and done. There was one episode that featured a girl who cut herself with razor blades whenever she felt overwhelmed.

She described it the way I'd heard other addicts describe heroin: like a lover, like the greatest feeling ever, like a warm light at the end of a bitter day. That was what I wanted. I had only had a taste of it and wanted more. That afternoon, on my way home from school, I biked to the drugstore and picked up old-school razor blades. So as not to look conspicuous, I also grabbed a pack of gum and a People magazine. That was the beginning of my love affair.

"You did more than cut yourself."

"Yeah. It really started with a razor blade."

What landed me in the hospital was the lighter. I never meant for things to go as far as they went. I had a hard time explaining that to everyone.

CHAPTER 20

On the Blue Ridge

It was still pretty dark, and the adrenaline that had fueled my muscles into flight was draining out of my body. The very real feeling of Kenny's hands on me left my legs shaky. Or was that my lack of sleep, lack of water, lack of food…

My thoughts bounced all over my brain, a confused jumble, and I felt my pace slow a little.

Why, I wondered, had Kenny chosen me to mess with? What about me told him he could? What about me told disgusting Mr. Carson he could try to kiss me? How did kids at school know they could attack me and get away with it?

It's because there's something wrong with you. Maybe there really is a root on you.

That old voice in my brain again, unwelcome. I tried to shut it down, tried to challenge it with true thoughts, but I was just so tired.

If you were normal, your dad would have stayed. If you were normal, your mom wouldn't have died.

He did it because he knew I wouldn't fight. *I* knew I wouldn't fight. The only person I'd ever fought against was myself.

You deserve all the shit you get. Why do you think you're out here right now, in the middle of the night, running your guts out? Because you deserve it.

My head started to swim. It felt disconnected from my body. I was nauseous but couldn't see far enough in front of me to throw up. My legs felt so heavy, and darkness edged out the corners of my vision. A cold wash of sweat covered my arms and legs, which suddenly refused to move another inch. The last words I heard before I hit the ground were these:

She's going to find you now.

• • •

At once, something cracks wide open and I am aloft, buoyed by an invisible wind. Untroubled by the memory of rising, I skim above the scene; weightless, hovering. Everything is beautiful. The land-scape is on fire with color; maples blazing red and yellow, bright like torches but not consumed. From above I feel all of it—every grain of dirt, each mossy rock—alive in the bones of my fingers. I stretch forward, testing movement, and understand that I should be still. My neck pulses, but there is no time for uncertainty or fear. My place is here, in the breathing, brutal sun.

There is no water here, not above nor below. My brain buzzes with the emptiness. It is hollowed-out, scooped clean, and burning like the untended pasture below me. I am at peace.

Suddenly, the impossible stirring of something alive. The scent I might have missed before, the scratch of nails on dry dirt. Shimmering from behind the rocks, a flash of white fur. A spark of clear blue eyes.

"I knew you'd come for me," I whisper, tasting air, feeling it underneath my wings, allowing my eyelids to fall for the first time. "I knew you'd come."

. . .

I woke up panicked, drenched in sweat, and with my left knee throbbing and my foot on fire. I still tasted the dream on my dry tongue, but my overwhelming need pushed it down. The plastic water bottle Lawrence had given me was half-full by my side.

You need water.

Forcing myself up on my elbows, looking at my surroundings, now partially lit by the rising sun, my mouth was so dry I could hardly swallow. My head throbbed from dehydration. I'd gulped down half the water bottle in Lawrence's truck, certain I was about to be rescued.

What are you going to do now?

I gingerly put my hands underneath my lower back where I'd fallen in the mossy grass and tried to think. Which way should I go?

You've studied maps of the relay for months now. You've got to find landmarks and figure out where you are.

I took a deep breath, assessing the damage to my body with detachment like I used to.

Dehydration.

Injured foot.

Severe headache.

Confusion.

A cold trail of fear snaked down my spine when I thought of Lorraine hunting me, but I shook it off. I allowed myself one small sip from the half-empty bottle before starting to run again.

If you don't get more water soon, you won't make it. You've got to find water.

I didn't slow my pace for what felt like about five off-road miles. By that point, the sun had lit up the sky in burnt orange and purple waves. It was beautiful, so I said it out loud. Catherine was always telling me that gratitude is the antidote for misery, so even though it felt stupid I said it.

"I'm thankful for the sun that rose today. I'm thankful for the light to see."

I knew I'd feel a lot more grateful without the overwhelming thirst that was clawing at my throat. I knew I had to find some water, but I was afraid to run too close to the road. The road's dangers were known—Kenny, Lorraine—and the off roads were unknown—bears and wild dogs and God-knew-what-else. I'd chosen the unknown and only encountered some high grass and a few holes. Without water, though, I'd never survive.

I remembered reading on the websites Brian had sent us that drinking stream water could lead to something called giardia, a parasite that could make you really sick. The last thing I needed to add to my troubles was stomach cramps and diarrhea, but I thought I might just need to take that risk.

Think, Bright. Where can you find clean water?

Clean water came from springs. It came from faucets. It came from the sky. I didn't see any clean water anywhere near me. I'd just have to keep looking.

CHAPTER 21

In Raleigh, After

"So, what do you know about your biological father."

"Not much. He's Cherokee. Or that's what my mom told me, anyway."

Catherine nodded, encouraging me.

My mother didn't tell me much about him, but what she did say stuck in my mind like a bedtime story. He was tall, he was quiet, he was kind, he was dark. My mom would repeat that sentence often—he was dark—and when I was little I thought this was because she wanted me to understand the color of my skin, or, rather, the color my skin wasn't. My mom was fair and wispy haired and my opposite physically, but I don't think my appearance bothered me much until she got me thinking about it.

Then, that thing happened that always happens when you are suddenly aware of something you should be ashamed of: other people picked up on it. Before I started school, I didn't think much about either my brown skin or my missing father.

Lots of kids had divorced parents. I knew my mom loved me, and I had neighborhood friends. Daniel next door would always come to our house after school, asking me to ride bikes. We'd ride as far as the neighborhood entrance, then fly back down the hill toward our street and repeat the trip all over again. When we were a little older, we'd bring our allowances and ride to the drugstore, buying lollipops and sodas and drinking them in the parking lot, wondering if the "No Loitering" signs applied to us.

"Even without a dad, things were normal when I was little."

I stopped for a moment, wondering how much to say.

"This girl Mary Bliss also lived on my street. She and I would go swimming at the neighborhood pool in the summertime. She had a hot pink bike with a basket, and we'd put our towels and her sunscreen—I never used it—into the basket as we rode. Our parents' only request was that we come home by dark, which we almost always did."

Catherine cocked her head toward me. "When did things change? When did they get harder for you?"

"I don't know. I guess around fourth grade."

Daniel had started playing baseball and his afternoons were full of practices and games and tournaments and homework. Plus, I was a girl, and by that age boys and girls didn't really play together after school. Then one day Mary Bliss became M.B. and started sitting with a different group of girls in the cafeteria—the girls who took ballet and cheerleading lessons, the girls whose hair ribbons always matched their socks, who shopped at the mall and wore nail polish. At first,

M.B. invited me to sit with them. When I brought a hummus sandwich and this girl Lorelei wrinkled her perfect, tiny little nose at me, saying, "What on earth is that smell?", leaning to whisper in M.B.'s ear while never once taking her eyes off me, I knew I was out. I knew my friendship with M.B. was over. And I didn't really know what to do next.

Until I met Brenda five years later after I'd been alone so long I almost didn't care anymore. When I'd already started cutting. When I was fully into my garbage art and running and hurting myself and I really didn't think I cared anymore about much of anything. I'd been out hunting for trash after school one day, killing time in the dusk before Kent got home from work, and I'd thought I was totally alone in my thoughts.

"Wait up." Her voice had made me jump three inches off the ground. I'd turned around and seen Brenda, slightly out of breath but clearly talking to me (there was no one else around), a big smile on her face. I recognized her. Our school wasn't big enough to be unrecognizable, unfortunately, but Brenda was pretty new. We'd never talked to each other. I couldn't imagine why she was following me now when I wanted more than anything to gather garbage in peace.

Jesus, what does she want?

"Whatcha doing?" Brenda let her eyes drop to the trash I held in my hands. I'd waited for her to wrinkle her nose; get grossed out. I noticed she wearing unfashionable jeans—what people called "Mom jeans" back then—and that her bangs clung to her forehead in greasy spikes. But her face was nice. She smiled at me.

"Oh, cool. A service project. Let me help." Just like that, she bent over at the waist, her already slightly high-water jeans rising even higher on her ankles, and started grabbing at trash. Brenda hadn't asked if she could help, she'd just begun. She ran in first one direction and then the other, eyes all over the grass, searching for garbage. She moved like a squirrel, starting a pile near my feet.

"Do you have a bag?" Her eyes were wide and bright green. For the first time, I'd realized that she wasn't making fun of me. My default reaction was suspicion, but she'd really wanted to help. I held a white bag out to her, still aware that I hadn't said a word. Just as quietly, she dropped the trash she'd gathered into the bag.

"I don't get it, do you? Why people would just throw their garbage in the grass—like they expect somebody to pick up after them?" Brenda spoke so fast and her speech was accented. I couldn't figure the accent out at first, but there was something there. She also had a lisp.

"You're a good person, Bright. Really. A good person." She tucked a strand of thin blond hair behind her ear and dropped to her knees, seemingly unaware that her jeans were instantly muddy from the damp grass.

We worked in silence for a while. Maybe 15 minutes passed before Brenda spoke again.

"Do you think maybe sometime you could show me how you do your makeup?" I'd been so surprised by the question that I'd laughed. I actually wasn't sure I'd heard her correctly.

"Oh, sorry. No. It's okay. You don't need to." Her cheeks blushed bright red. My laughter had offended her.

"No, I'm not laughing at you. I'm confused." I'd stammered a little. Surely, she could tell I wasn't making fun of her.

"Your makeup. I love how you do your eyeliner. I'm hopeless when it comes to makeup." *Hopeless* came out sounding like *hope-leth*.

"I don't wear makeup." My voice had sounded rude, even to me.

"Oh, gosh, I'm sorry." Brenda's full cheeks burned even brighter, and she looked away from me immediately.

"No, no, it's okay—" I'd said at the same time Brenda had said, "It's just impossible that you are this pretty without makeup."

It was my turn to blush. People didn't typically describe me as "pretty."

"It's just how my eyes are, I guess. Dark around the edges. I've always thought it makes me look tired."

Brenda snorted. "I wish I looked 'tired' like you. I mean, Bright. Seriously. You look like you should be in a magazine."

Okay, maybe she was making fun of me.

"What kind of magazine, exactly?"

At that, Brenda laughed. Hard. She had one of those laughs that sounded like a balloon popping; the sound bursting out of her. It made me laugh, too.

"You're seriously hopeless." Again, "hope-leth." She shook her head. "Skinny, tall, perfect skin, thick hair…some people don't appreciate their God-given gifts." She looked down at her thighs as she squatted. "I mean, I'm never going to be anything but chubby and pale."

Were we really doing this? Were we doing the girly "I'm-so-fat-no-I'm-so-fat" routine?

I stayed quiet.

"It's cool, though. I'm really good at math." And then that laugh again, like a cork popping off a champagne bottle. She reached out and shoved my shoulder a little, and I laughed even harder. Brenda wasn't like the other girls at school; not even close. I could like this girl, I thought to myself. She could be my friend.

She was, as it turns out. She helped me with math homework from that day forward. I laughed at her jokes and walked her home from school. She still gets mad at me for not opening up to her. She still teases me for being beautiful and hopeless. She still has the faintest accent and the tiniest lisp, especially when she is tired. Most importantly, Brenda would have been there for me when I was in the hospital. She wanted to be. But I never texted her. I never let her know where I was. When Kent found my phone and had me unlock it, I had 43 texts from Brenda. She was pissed.

WHAT IN THE ACTUAL HELL, B? WHERE RU?

I'd known she was furious right away because she never cursed—not even "hell" or "damn" or "asshole." Other people at school thought it was because she was a prude or a Jesus freak, but she really just didn't like the way it sounded. Brenda's family had moved to the US from Serbia when she was only six and her real name wasn't Brenda. Though she spoke

English well, she once told me she didn't have time to learn words that weren't going to do her any good. She was different from every other girl I had ever met. And she wanted to be my friend, not in spite of the fact that I was gathering trash, but because of it.

It's not like we were the joint outcasts, Bright and Brenda against the world. Nothing like that. Brenda had her own friends. She was involved in school stuff—the debate team, honor choir, French Club—and she took hip-hop classes on the weekends. She had a big, loud family. She stayed really busy all of the time, but she always checked in with me. She had made my life better.

I took a deep breath, suddenly feeling irritable. "Anyway, that was sort of how it went. Is this even important? From third grade until now, I've pretty much been alone except Brenda."

I've been alone more often than I've been with people, if I really think about it. Being alone and running go hand in hand, though. I mean, I don't think I'd be able to run long distances by myself like I do, if I were always worried about other people. I see how these girls are. I see how they can't take a step without asking their friends what they are doing, wearing, eating, watching. Without checking their phones to see what they might be missing. Being alone feels like it's in my DNA. In my head, I've connected being alone with being Cherokee. And never did my ability to be alone mean more than when I was running through the mountains. There was no one to help me, and I tried to imagine what my ancestors might have felt when they were alone, hunted, afraid. What saved them? Nature? Prayer? God? Their ancestors?

"You're here now, Bright. You tell me. Is it important? Is any of it important?"

CHAPTER 22

On the Blue Ridge

The temperature was perfect, I suddenly realized. It was warmer than it should've been in the mountains at that time of year, which meant I wasn't freezing my sweat-soaked bones. The hoodie made a difference, too, zipped all the way up to my chin.

The only sound I heard was the rhythmic crush of my running shoes hitting the mulchy ground. The sky was getting lighter by the moment, on fire with color. My eyes felt unfocused, my head detached from my neck. I looked up and there it was: The hawk, its wings spread as wide as the sky, soaring above me. Once, twice. Was it real? The bird was so large and so close and came upon me so suddenly that I stopped running for a moment to stare at it. Could this be the same hawk I'd seen a lifetime ago, back at the Mountain Inn? In a way I couldn't really describe, it felt like the soaring silhouette knew me. Was it following me, watching out for me?

Thank you, hawk.

As I stopped to catch my breath, the hawk soared again. Really, I just saw his outline—wide and dark, with long brown wings making a smooth arc above me, pinned against a sky on fire. It was inviting me to follow. If anyone knew how to stay alive out here on the Blue Ridge, it was the hawk, so I had no choice but to try to keep up.

Remember your dream.

For a moment, as I was still, staring at this incredible creature in the sky, I felt absolute clarity.

In your dream, you were the hawk. You are the hawk.

I was the hawk. I didn't feel the exhaustion soaking my bones or my parched throat; I just stared at the sky, thinking.

Maybe you know where you're going. Maybe you are going to be okay.

Crazy as it was, it was this thought that pushed me to find a road, or some civilization, in spite of my fear. I momentarily wished for my missing GPS watch, but maybe not knowing how far I'd run wasn't the worst thing.

Without thinking, I rolled up my sleeves and traced my fingertips over the peaked scars of my forearms. My stomach folded in on itself with guilt. Thinking of Kent's eyes when he saw me lying in that hospital bed. Remembering his plaintive, "Why?" as he held me by the shoulders, my arms wrapped in bandages.

I'd already hurt him so much. And now this.

Why?

The question burned on my tongue as I ran, steady but slower, toward what felt like the light. Catherine had never been as direct as Kent in her questions, allowing the "therapeutic process," as she called it, to "unfold," but she had wanted to know, too.

"You set yourself on fire, Bright," she'd said to me after we'd been meeting for several months and she knew I could handle it, "what made you do that? What was going on in your head that day?"

As I thought about it, my pace slowed more. This always happened to me: think negative thoughts, dwell on bad memories, and lose physical momentum. Still, I couldn't help myself. When I was talking to Catherine, I had said, "The lighter was on my dresser. The nail polish remover was right next to it because I'd just taken off my toenail polish. They were both right there in front of me. What played out in my head that day were the same thoughts that had played out in my head so many times before, but the pain was just so much greater at that moment. Things just got out of hand."

Because the truth, which gradually came out, is that I'm covered with scars. Inside, outside, arms, legs, heart. I've been hurting myself for so long I can't even explain why I did it, why I do it. Running on a rock or poking myself with glass or pushing myself past the point of exhaustion? It's all self-injury. Running is just socially acceptable and rarely lands people in the hospital.

I was snapped out of my thoughts by the sound of a large vehicle approaching. I immediately ran toward the sound, guessing it was an eighteen-wheeler or a construction truck. It was loud enough to pull me toward it, and I sprinted in spite of my exhaustion, in spite of my thirst. My body took over and hurled itself through time, breaking through the air like a knife. Then, I was waving my arms like a crazy person, I was screaming, I was thinking about nothing other than GETME-OUTOFHERE. I was crying.

Please, pleasepleaseplease take me home.

It was a mantra, it was coiling through my brain, it was taking me over.

Please please please.

But the truck rambled on, unseeing, leaving me alone again.

. . .

SESSION #: 5
DATE: JULY 25
TIME: 9:30 A.M.
CATHERINE M. SONDLER, LCSW

Client again arrived early for session; this time almost 20 minutes early. Client had colored and cut her hair. Previously dark brown, long, and straight, now pale blond, short, and curly. When asked about the new hairstyle, client became angry but spoke in a little-girl voice, "Can't a girl give herself a makeover?" Affect suggested mania. Client appeared unable to sit still and speech was rapid and pressured. When questioned about medication compliance and any changes in lifestyle, client laughed inappropriately. "You'd like it if

I kept taking them pills, wouldn't you?" she responded. I indicated that, yes, I would like client to maintain the medication regimen prescribed by her doctor. While I outlined the negative consequences of stopping medication abruptly, client interrupted and told me she didn't think she needed the pills. Asked if anything had happened to cause client to stop taking her medication, and client rose from her chair and began pacing the office.

With no tearful affect or emotional reaction, client shared that her husband had left her. Client suggested that perhaps the pills were making her worse instead of better, and maybe that's why her husband had left. There was only one way to find out, she indicated. Client continued pressured, incoherent speech as she paced around the room and attempts to calm her failed. At one point, client shouted, "I wish you'd just tell me what to do!" When probed further, client appeared to become angry. Despite protestations, client left the office and slammed the door behind her.

CHAPTER 23

In Raleigh, After

"The thing no one tells you is that life is so big." For a moment, I wasn't sure if I'd said this out loud to Catherine or merely thought it.

"What do you mean?"

The strangest thing about my time on the Blue Ridge was that for the past ten years, I'd dreamed of a similar scenario. I had hoped and prayed and wished to be left alone, to be released, to be entirely by myself without anyone to answer to.

"When Kent was, like, catatonic with grief, I remember wishing I could just get away from him. When I left the hospital, I wondered what would happen if I just kept going, ran away, never went back home. I'm not sure why I never did. What I do know is that being totally alone didn't feel like I thought it might."

"How do you mean?"

"I don't know. I guess it didn't feel like freedom. It felt like being cut off. At least, at first."

At the beginning, it seemed like all I'd wished for turned out to be an illusion; smoke and ashes. Dust. But maybe that's just me. Running through the darkness, I tried to remember what tethered me to the earth—my ancestors, my history. I remembered good things. I thought of Levi and "Star light, star bright." When I did that, I felt a little less alone.

CHAPTER 24

On the Blue Ridge

If you don't sleep, you will die.

I decided this as my run slowed to a jog; at first imperceptibly, then without question. I had to sleep. I was terrified to sleep. I wasn't sure what time it was, but the sky was deep blue, and its darkness had crept into my brain. It was infecting my thoughts.

Things will look better after you sleep.

I stopped completely, trying to orient myself among the dark pines. The woods were alive with sounds and smells. The forest floor shook and scattered. A slight wind swayed the pines and my lungs filled with their scent. As I exhaled, my legs nearly collapsed from exhaustion.

"When you need to rest, rest. When you need to eat, eat. Your only job on this planet, Bright, is to just be."

Catherine's voice was as clear as water, rushing over me, soothing me. How many times had she told me this; that my only job is to be? And there I was, in the middle of a haunted mountain, trying to take her advice and wondering if it was the worst I'd ever heard. I had no choice, though. If I didn't sleep, I was going to die. I was shaking so much I couldn't imagine calming down enough to sleep. I lay down on the cold ground, damp with fallen leaves, and the world turned off.

. . .

I'm blind, but I know it is because I'm blindfolded. I'm sitting on a rock, or a stump, in the middle of the forest. It's cold, but I know not to shiver. I hear the forest sounds, the rustling in the trees of the night animals, the faint hooting of an owl, branches swayed by the night wind. I smell autumn: damp leaves, moss, the slightest hint of wood burning.

I know I must sit here all night, all by myself, until the sun rises again. This is how I'll become a Cherokee woman. I must prove my strength and courage. I can't cry out; I can't remove the blindfold. The only way to earn my place is to be brave. I will do it.

An eternity passes and I'm so afraid, but I don't touch the blindfold. I don't dare remove it. Somehow, I know it's so much more important to survive this. I know I will feel proud of myself when it's all over.

I hear the heavy footsteps of an animal; a big one. A low noise. It's moving closer and closer toward me. I'm terrified. So close to ripping the blindfold off and running, jumping into a tree, doing whatever I can to get away. I can almost feel the animal's breath on me. I'm close to panic.

Then the crack of a gunshot.

It's not me—I'm not hurt. I can tell, though, from the light filtering through the blindfold, that night is over. I've made it. I tear the blindfold from my face and I can see.

Before me stands my father, a rifle by his side, and the body of a dead bear.

"I've been beside you all along," he says, his brown eyes filled with tears. "I will never leave you. Remember that. You are never alone."

I woke up with a start.

There was another crack. The gunshots weren't just in my dream. They were real.

Someone was shooting.

. . .

SESSION #: 6
DATE: AUGUST 1
TIME: 9:30 A.M.
CATHERINE M. SONDLER, LCSW

No show. Client called after the session to reschedule, stating she'd forgotten the appointment. Her speech was again pressured, and client sounded manic. Client stated she'd been working on an important project that had her waking up early and staying up late. When asked how much sleep she'd been getting, client stated that she hadn't slept in a few days but would be sleeping that evening. When asked if she'd been taking her medication as prescribed, client hung up the phone with no response.

CHAPTER 25

On the Blue Ridge

Lorraine's found you and she's shooting at you. This is it. You're dead.

I took off running blindly, no destination in sight. It looked to be almost dawn, and I could make out where my feet were falling. I was freezing. How long had I slept?

And another crack.

The shot felt too close to my head, so I ran in a crouch. Speed was impossible, but at least I felt safer from the bullets.

From the bullets.

What in the hell are you doing? You can't outrun a gun. Just stop. Aren't you tired? Just lie down. It'll be so much easier.

The voice in my head reminded me of the times I thought dying might be easier. There had been a few. Even though hurting myself never started out as wanting to die, it sure did numb the pain of living. And I couldn't count the number of times, especially right after my mom died, that I thought about joining her. I didn't actually want to die, I just wanted the pain to stop. Before I ever seriously considered it, anyway, the thought of my mom *knowing* I'd killed myself stopped me. Imagining the look on her face—would I ever even see her face?—when she learned that I'd taken the easy way out was too much for me. After all the fighting she did to stay alive for me, I imagined she'd be pretty pissed at me for giving up.

"I'm a different person now than I was then. I've learned a lot from Catherine. I've learned a lot about what is my responsibility and what isn't. I will see Kent and Aunt Laura and Catherine and Brenda again." I whispered this to myself, gasping for breath and feeling like I'd lost my mind. Pain seared my foot with every step, but I couldn't stop moving. I had to do whatever I could to stay alive.

What if what you think is true isn't actually true?

The voice in my head startled me so much that I slowed my pace.

What if the gunshots are coming from hunters? There are deer in these woods, surely, and rabbits and squirrels ...What if behind the gun is someone who can help you?

I slowed down even more. What if it wasn't Lorraine firing the gun, but someone else? Someone who could help? What if I were to run *toward* the gun shots? I stopped for a millisecond to weigh my options.

I turned on my heel and ran toward the sound.

"Hey!" I shouted, as assertively as I could.

"Hey! I need help!" my voice was raw and unfamiliar. Through the growing light, I saw a figure—a man—running away from me.

"Hey! Don't go! Stop running!" *Why is he running?* "Please help me!" My last plea was a sob, caught in my chest, ragged and pathetic.

But, like a ghost, he evaporated into the thick trees.

I covered my face with my hands, fighting to keep my tears inside. Maybe he was homeless, poaching for survival. Maybe he was as scared of me as I was of him. Maybe he thought he had shot me?

I stopped fighting, then I let myself scream. It was a low, animal wail—my throat was so dry I could barely make any more sound; my lungs were on fire—but somehow, it made me feel a little better. I curled into a ball, overcome by the effort of screaming.

What now? What in the hell are you going to do now?

· · ·

CALL LOG:
DATE: AUGUST 4
TIME: 10:00 A.M.
CATHERINE M. SONDLER, LCSW

Attempted to contact client with no answer. Left voicemail for client on her cell phone.

CHAPTER 26

In Raleigh, After

"You said music helped you survive. What did you mean?"

"Music is really important to me. I get that most people my age like pop music, or hip-hop, or rock. I hardly know anyone who's into old time or bluegrass."

I laughed a little, wondering what kind of music Catherine listened to. Her face was a blank canvas, a lot like her office. I looked around at the featureless beige walls and the Ikea bookshelves lined with titles like *The Courage to Heal* and *Feeling Good*.

Courage? Ha.

In my 7th grade Music Appreciation class we each had to write a report and give an oral presentation on our favorite style of music. The teacher had to limit the number of kids who chose rock and roll and pop, but most of the other kids thought bluegrass was just nasal, twangy crap some of their parents listened to.

"My seventh-grade music teacher, Mrs. Millstone, totally freaked out when I told her I was into bluegrass."

Her face had lit up and I think she may have even clapped her hands together when I said it. I remembered her face so clearly. She had these granny glasses she was always pushing up on her nose.

She'd said, "You know, much of today's popular music has its roots in bluegrass and mountain music." She'd said that like I didn't know it. She'd told me how she and her husband were big into old-time music; how he played the mandolin in parking lots and campgrounds at bluegrass festivals all over the state.

"How did that feel for you, to be heard?"

"God. Seriously? So embarrassing. She was so lame, that teacher everyone made fun of, and I just remember staring at her because I didn't know what to say."

But, oh, did I love bluegrass. When I was about five years old, my Aunt Laura started playing Alison Krauss in the car and, corny as it sounds, I thought I'd heard an angel sing. Her voice—totally like she was from another space and time—overtook me. I couldn't get enough of her music. Somehow, through Alison I learned of other artists: I spent some time completely obsessed with Ralph Stanley and Earl Scruggs.

"But I love bluegrass. I love it all. I love the—" I raised my eyebrows, "—authenticity of it. I love the fact that it's accessible to everyone. When I'm alone, I sometimes sing along."

I felt embarrassed that I'd confessed this to Catherine.

Not that anybody knows that I sing. I have a terrible voice, but when I hear a song I love, especially one about heartache and loss and grief that guts me, I *need* to sing along. Once, in Mrs. Millstone's class, we did this unit on jazz music. That clueless teacher made each of us—seventh graders—scat sing a solo in front of the class. I was mortified and thought I wouldn't live through it. I waited as the other kids, equally red-faced and terrified, be-bop-a-loued for a few moments. Then it was my turn.

My mouth was dry. I could hardly think. The music played on and I was, just, silent. After several awkward moments, I finally made an attempt that sounded exactly like…"barf." From that day on, all the kids in MA class made barfing noises at me whenever the teacher had her back turned. By that point, I'd been terrorized for so long, you'd think it wouldn't have bothered me. But something about the fact that I'd embarrassed myself in music class, when music was something I loved so much, made it sting even more. That was probably the first and last time I've ever sung in public.

CHAPTER 27

On the Blue Ridge

The damp settled around me like a blanket. Pain shot through my head. My foot felt like it was broken. My calves were burning, and I was thirstier than I could ever remember having been. I'd drink a gallon of cold coffee right now, a gallon of toilet water, a gallon of Scotch, I thought. I was so thirsty, and so alone. I allowed myself one more tiny sip of water from the plastic bottle I'd gotten from Lawrence. With no one around me, no one to judge, I decided to sing. I started with the old bluegrass I love so much.

> *I was standing by the window*
> *On one cold and cloudy day*
> *When I saw the hearse come rolling*
> *For to carry my mother away*

I'd begun singing this song in my quiet, off-key voice, its notes carrying out into the dark mountain landscape, without thinking about the words. I heard the soft sound of my running shoes on the pine-covered ground. I kept singing.

Will the circle be unbroken
By and by Lord, by and by
There's a better home awaiting
In the sky Lord, in the sky

I thought of a better home, wondering for the millionth time where my father was; if he was living or dead. Did he see me now? Was he carrying me along through the forest, through the darkness? Was he helping me, shooting down my attackers overnight?

I said to the undertaker
Undertaker please drive slow
For this lady you are carrying
Lord I hate to see her go

When my mom died, I was so angry. I couldn't believe in anything, because believing in God meant acknowledging that God didn't give a shit about me—I didn't even deserve a mother. But now? I wasn't so sure. I had a tough time imagining my mom in a sea of black forever. I couldn't believe that everyone who counted on some kind of afterlife was just wrong.

Oh, I followed close behind her
Tried to hold up and be brave
But I could not hide my sorrow
When they laid her in the grave
Will the circle be unbroken
By and by Lord, by and by
There's a better home awaiting
In the sky Lord, in the sky

Running and singing in the middle of the living Blue Ridge, breathing the thin air, tears streaming down my face, holding the moment close to my chest, I repeated, with every step I took, like a mantra, what that camp counselor Britt had told me years ago: "I was her light."

The thing is, I know it doesn't make any sense at all, but somehow singing this sad, spiritual song made me feel better; made me run faster. It shouldn't have. My voice is terrible and the words to the song? Like I've said, I'm not sure I even believe them. But whether it was the act of singing, or the memory of my life at home, or the mere distraction of music instead of just feet pounding on ground, I felt better.

And then the rain came, almost like I'd called it.

It was like a rustle in the treetops at first, making me wonder what kind of bird was nesting up there. The drops started slowly, but when I say it started to rain, I need you to understand that it started to *pour*. It was that kind of dousing rain that actually hurts your neck and shoulders, stings your face, soaks you through with its force. I'd run in rain before, I thought I liked running in the rain, in fact, but this was rain like I'd never experienced. I just opened up my mouth and let it pour down my parched throat. I stopped for a good five minutes just to drink the rain. I held up my plastic bottle and let it fill with rain, drinking it and letting it fill again. My hair was sticking to my forehead; my shirt glued to my back. My running shoes started to slide a little on the ground which seemed to shift with every step. I tried not to think about what kind of blisters I'd have if I made it through this day. Still, I kept singing.

As I was about to begin another round, I noticed the outline of something up ahead, rising out of the mountain mist, sprung up from nowhere on the overgrown trail. Off behind a large tree, it looked like a man-made shed or a lean-to or something, the lines of its roof rising through the gray light. For a moment, I had to wonder if I was hallucinating. I mean, I was exhausted, and what, after all, were the odds that I'd stumble upon a shelter in the middle of nowhere at the beginning of a torrential storm? I sprinted toward it, not even thinking about what might be inside, about who might be inside, about where I was going. I needed to touch its walls, smell it. I needed to know it was real.

All I could think about was, if it *was* real, maybe people were near. As I approached the shed, I allowed myself to slow down a little. There was no light inside. There was no door knob or anything, just a hole where a door knob ought to be on a rotting wooden door. Slowly, gingerly, I placed my fingers through the hole and pulled the door toward me. There was an ungodly creak, shattering the rain's rhythmic patter like a sledgehammer. It was dark in the shack, but a small cracked window let some gray light, as well as a lot of rainwater, in. I saw no sign a human had been there. I did see what appeared to be a dirt floor, some scrap wood in the corner, loads of cobwebs, and not much else. A thought suddenly occurred to me: I could sleep here. Just for a few hours. I could elevate my foot and gather my strength a little. I could let myself be sheltered.

I spotted an old earthenware jug in the corner of the shack. It looked like it could've contained anything—motor oil, bacon grease, who knows—but, what was it I'd thought earlier?

I'd drink a gallon of toilet water.

Despite the rainwater I'd drunk, I was overcome with thirst; an animal drive. I lifted the jug to my face, shaking it slightly to see if any liquid was inside. Something sloshed. I put it to my nose and sniffed.

The foulest, moldiest odor I'd ever smelled flooded my brain.

Don't throw up. Don't throw up.

I could barely keep it together and had to stick my head back outside of the shack, back into the pelting rain, to get a full breath of fresh air. I counted to eight on my in-breath, eight on my out-breath, letting the rainwater flood my open mouth. Catherine used to tell me to breathe when I needed to calm down. Eight on in-breath, Eight on out-breath. After a few cycles, I could safely go back inside the shack without puking. I let the rain wash the jug out, dumping it once, twice, three times. I left it outside to fill with rain alongside my bottle.

In spite of the rain, it was getting lighter outside by the moment.

Keep your head about you, Bright. You're going to be okay. You just need to rest.

My head felt foggy, white dots appearing before my eyes. With all my body and mind had been through, more rest was what I needed. Propping my leg against the wall in the corner of that damp, dirty shed, I was shocked by how quickly I could just let go of my reality, let go of everything, and sleep.

It was dark when I woke up with a jolt, and eerily quiet: no sounds, no birds. Just silent. For a moment, I wondered what could have woken me. Slowly, I sat up, feeling every sore muscle and bruise on my body, stretching my neck, looking from side to side. I'd slept flat on my back, shoulders scrunched up to my ears, with my foot elevated. I was so cold I was shaking, my damp clothes clinging to me, my toes soggy—likely blistered—in their socks. Then, a scratching noise broke the quiet. It sounded like someone was trying to open the door of the shed.

Someone? Something?

I scrambled to my feet, still dazed, noticing the aches all over my body. With nothing between my hoodie and the rough ground, I'd been jabbed by rocks and uneven ground for the last few hours. I tried to stand up straight; tried to force alertness.

How amazing would a hot cup of coffee be right now?

I know it was a weird thought to have, but for a few seconds, I gave in to the fantasy, thinking of the last cup I'd drunk before the relay started. Like so many things in my life, I hadn't appreciated it enough at the time. Only now, with no hope for any coffee any time soon, did I honor the simple gift of a hot cup. Or a quinoa salad. Or even those crappy baked beans Lorraine had given me.

Lorraine. She's here. Focus.

She'd found me. Somehow, she'd tracked me to this hovel, she'd gone off road in her hatchback and she'd sniffed me out like a bloodhound. My heart pounded in my chest.

Or, it's an animal.

The rain had slowed, highlighting how quiet it was outside the shed. It was nearly silent. The birds and bugs of the forest were completely quiet, which seemed strange. There wasn't much light, but now that the rain had calmed and all was quiet, I decided, I should get out of there. I peered through the small window, almost absently, not really sure what I was looking for but feeling unnerved by so much quiet.

Just then, an incredible weight came crashing toward me, first blocking the window, then cracking the glass further, ripping the silence in half. I jumped back from the window as quickly as I could, making a noise like a trapped animal.

Thick, dark fur. Heavy body.

It wasn't possible. Was it possible?

Could there actually be a bear trying to get into this shed?

Think, Bright. Think.

I took a deep breath, willing the buzz in my ears to quiet. Breathing in again, I felt like I could pass out if I allowed myself to. I commanded myself to remember. I had read up on bears, on mountain lions, on wild dogs, on all kinds of wildlife before I left for the relay.

Remember, God damn it.

Before the relay. Man, that felt like a lifetime ago. A time when I used a hairbrush and took showers and had hot coffee in the mornings. How long had I been gone? I thought for a moment...maybe two days? Three? Had Kent missed me? Had Laura? A lump rose in my throat.

Will you ever find your way home?

I pictured Catherine's stop sign in my mind again, rubbing my eyes. I had immediate problems to deal with.

Black bears want food.

Calmer now, I remembered. They don't usually attack people unless they think they are prey. Unprovoked attacks are rare, and usually happen in remote areas where bears aren't used to seeing people. They like their own personal space.

This bear probably had no interest in me. Like me, he was probably hungry and searching for something. Like me, he was probably alone. When a black bear feels like his space is threatened, I remembered, he may paw the ground or act aggressively toward a human. If, after backing away slowly, he continues to approach, the human should make herself as big as possible and throw non-food objects at the bear.

Kent had made me watch a video about bears before the race. I remembered muttering, "This is ridiculous," under my breath, a Raleigh kid considering the presence of a bear about as likely as the appearance of an alien spaceship.

You're not so smart after all, are you?

The scratching got louder, and I weighed my options. Hide and pretend and wait, or confront and stake claim? I tried my best to remember everything I could about the black bear.

He could enter the shed. He could kill you if he wanted to.

Or he might need direction. He could need me to tell him there's no food in here, he shouldn't waste his time.

I can't be certain what I was thinking in those moments, but I know I thought some version of this: Fear of a black bear is what led me off the relay trail in the first place. If I hadn't been so fearful, I never would've ended up in Lorraine's car, in Lorraine's cabin, in this situation. My fear had made my decision for me.

No more.

I shouted at the absolute top of my lungs.

"GO AWAY!" I stomped my feet and pounded on the shed's walls. Adrenaline coursed through my arms and legs. I suddenly felt superhuman.

"Go away! There's nothing for you here! Get lost!" I pounded my fists against the thin walls of the shed, shouting as loudly as my voice would carry.

"Get the hell out of here!" There was a rush and a crash, and the glass on the ancient window shattered. Broken glass sprayed around my shoulders, but I didn't feel anything.

My breathing was so shallow I again worried I might faint. I found myself holding it in; waiting.

Silence.

Not a crack of a tree branch. Not a leaf blowing in the night wind. Silence.

I counted to 50.

Still silent.

"Well, I'll be damned."

I broke the silence and looked down at my scraped and muddied torso, not seeing blood, and not feeling pain.

As soon as it had come, the bear was gone. As suddenly as it had taken over the shed, as suddenly as it terrified me, it was no longer there.

Was it ever there at all? How can you be sure? Maybe you imagined the whole thing.

No.

When I was in the hospital, the counselors taught us to go through this process to analyze self-limiting or self-harming thoughts. We were supposed to ask, "Is it true? Do I know for sure that it's true? What evidence do I have to support this belief?" when challenging our critical thinking. Nine times out of ten, as it turns out, the ugly things we think about and say to ourselves aren't even true. They don't even pass the first test. So, I considered this when I thought about the bear. Was it here? Yes. How can I be sure it was here? I saw its paw, I heard its clatter, I smelled its presence. The drugs that Lorraine gave me surely affected my senses—I don't doubt that—but what I found even more troubling about them is that they made me doubt my sanity. We all see and hear things when we are terrified, but I knew, *I know* that the bear was real. I'd swear to it.

All that shouting. I was so thirsty.

Go outside. The jug is still outside.

I walked outside to get my rainwater, scanning the ground for the jug. Something had knocked over the heavy jug, and it certainly hadn't been the wind. Water had spilled out all over the ground. The ground was saturated with it.

A bear was here. Again. A bear was here, it knocked over your water jug, and you drove it away.

• • •

Finn, N.C.—Authorities say seventeen-year-old runner Bright Shelby remains missing from the North Carolina Mountain Relay race route as of approximately 10:00 p.m. Saturday night. At press time, Miss Shelby has been missing for approximately 40 hours.

Jimmy Holden, the race's director, expressed his concern for the young runner. "We get several calls a year about missing runners. No one has ever stayed lost longer than a few hours, so we are very concerned about Bright. We're confident the sheriff's department will locate her soon."

Sheriff Cole Martinez said the race's rugged terrain has impeded the search process. "Anybody out here knows that radio reception is poor. Cell phones don't work. It's a heavily wooded course." The sheriff's department is urgently calling for volunteers to join in a foot search party for Miss Shelby. Those willing to join search efforts should contact the department at (828) 733-3000.

Sources indicate that Shelby has experienced mental and emotional problems in recent months. Audrey Christian, local high school English teacher, weighed in. "I just hope they find her alive. The woods are no place for a teenager alone, and knowing she has mental problems makes it that much more worrying."

Kent Shelby, Bright Shelby's stepfather, gave a statement last night. "We are so grateful to anyone willing to help us find Bright. She is loved and missed by many. Please come back to us safe, honey."

Shelby's family is offering a financial reward for her safe return. Anyone with any information about Bright Shelby's whereabouts should contact the sheriff's department at (828) 733-3000.

CHAPTER 28

On the Blue Ridge

I'd rested as much as I could, refilled the jug with rainwater, and drunk some more water. I knew I had to keep moving. The leaves crunched under my feet; the overt musky smell reminded me that I was surrounded by life—animals and bugs and trees and flowers—but I knew I was utterly alone. I remembered how many times I'd sat on my bed, the door closed even though Kent had no intention of coming to find me, staring at the wall, then assembling my art, then slicing at my arm with a razor blade, watching the bright red lines rise like kite strings, then staring at the wall again. Those times when I thought solitude and stillness equaled safety, when I had prayed to be far away from anyone who might bother me or hurt me. For the first time, I could see myself so clearly. There weren't just wounds on my arms—I was an open wound. Because I was desperate and sad and felt so unloved when I was around others, all I wanted was to be alone. But when I was alone, I was crueler to myself than anyone else had ever been. As I ran, the darkness lifting around my shoulders, tears came to my eyes.

"But why didn't you fight?" I said aloud, almost breathlessly. "Why didn't you ever fight back? Why did you only fight against yourself?" It was as if this thought had never occurred to me before—the idea that I could've stood up and fought back and stopped allowing people to hurt me; that I could've told them all to just leave me alone. Once this idea took root in my brain, though, it was impossible to shake. I was sprinting now. Frenzied.

"No more fighting yourself. No more." I kept going, faster and faster.

"From now on, you fight back!" I shouted this last sentence in a triumphant roar, giddy with my epiphany and lack of sleep and food. I was flying.

I was too deep in my own thoughts.

I saw the water too late.

Maybe the sound of the rain disguised it. The rushing of blood in my ears might have been too loud. My hunger and thirst and confusion might have been too great. Who knows, but I never really even heard the water, though it was there all along and I should have noticed. All I know is that I came upon what just looked like a small river; a stream. I made the split-second decision to just run through it. I thought the water would come up to my ankles or my knees. I didn't think there was an alternate route if I didn't cross. My shoes would get wet again, but they were already soaked from the rain. I was barreling forward so fast that I was afraid I wouldn't be able to stop running in time even if I wanted to.

Jump.

It was an instant decision, and it was a terrible one. I was underwater in a flash, everything tumbling, foot over head, rocks crashing elbows, scraping my shorts, head knocked against ground. What did I know about water? About nature? Who did I think I was?

Open your eyes. Breathe. Stay calm.

The water rushed so fast over me. So fast. I couldn't right myself. I couldn't tell which way was surface, which way was air.

I was panicking. I suddenly thought, "This might be how I die." Could it be? That after everything I'd been through, after my mom's death, after the fire, the injury, the hospital, the run, the abduction, the men, the gunshots, the bear...was it possible that a creek would be what took me down?

Hell. No.

"You got to learn how to fight," Granny Queen had said, "Or fightin'll be taught to you."

Fight. Don't stop fighting.

The water was everywhere. I tried to keep my eyes open.

"Star light, star bright, first star I see tonight..."

You were her light.

I had to keep kicking my legs. I had to look for the light.

Light.

I saw it above me and I grabbed at it with both hands, punching through the surface of the water like it was a glass window. I clawed at whatever was close and found a rock, a small handhold, and forced my body above the surface. I dragged my stomach onto the rock with everything I had, vomiting creek water, gasping at the air, grabbing at the air with my lungs, still alive, God damn it, my eyes toward the light.

You learned how to fight.

It had been taught to me.

· · ·

I thought I'd never catch my breath. I did my best to lie as still as possible, to expend as little energy as I could, while I gathered my strength. I stretched out on the bank of what I could now see was a raging river. How was it possible that I hadn't realized this before? The sun was bright now, and I slid off the hoodie to warm my arms and shoulders. I closed my eyes. I was so tired, an exhaustion like nothing I'd felt before. I was so tired I felt like crying. So tired I could hardly think straight; I knew I needed to fill up on the river water, I needed to take advantage of the water in front of me—giardia or not—but I was just so tired. A breeze cast its breath over me, gentle and reassuring, and I opened my eyes for just a moment. In that instant I saw the hawk—the same hawk, it had to be—hovering over me. Gliding and dipping, it took me a moment to realize he was writing a message to me in the sky. He was tracing a note to me, trying to communicate some private direction just to me. In white smoke, in what looked like skywriting, I saw the bird's message, curled above me: "Onward. To the light."

CHAPTER 29

In Raleigh, Before

"Did you ever ask for help, Bright? Did anyone ever notice you needed help?" Catherine's question almost made me cry, which is something I'd avoided doing in therapy up to that point.

"When I was a freshman, I wrote a poem that the guidance counselor interpreted as suicidal." I stopped talking for a second, unsure how much more I wanted to say. Then I went for it.

"That's the thing about art: it's gotten me into trouble as much as it's helped me. But I wouldn't abandon it for anything."

"Abandon. That's an interesting word."

"Yeah." I knew what Catherine meant. That's what my dad had done to me, although I tried not to think about it very often. Had he looked at me, eyes wide in his dark skin, and thought, "Oh, shit. This will not do. I've got to go." Or was it something that rolled and tumbled in his mind over days and weeks? Had he begun to understand the magnitude of 18 years of me? Had he realized that no one else was going to take over his job for him unless he left? Had he sniffed out my mom's impending death, somehow guessing that he'd be screwed over by me unless he got the hell out?

"Have you felt abandoned? In your life?"

I'd said too much already. I didn't respond to Catherine. The room was silent for a good three minutes.

"You've tried to meet your dad over the years, haven't you." It wasn't a question, so she must have known.

I'd nodded. "I always thought once I met my real dad, everything would be better. I'd find out he'd actually been looking for me all along." He hadn't abandoned me at all; instead, he'd lost my mom's contact info and had been unable to get in touch with us for my entire life. This fantasy, whenever I tried to construct it, just didn't work. There was the internet. My mom lived in the same city she'd always lived in. He knew my name. If he'd wanted me, he could've found me.

He didn't want me. But I so wanted him. When I was about 13, I decided I would track him down; quietly, without fuss. I'd find him.

I knew his name. I imagined he was untethered; no new wife, no real job, no other kids. I didn't know. But I knew his name and I figured I could track him down, so I did.

"I found an email address for him online—not connected to a job, a free URL."

I'd sat down at my laptop, at a loss for what to write.

Dear Dad: Why did you leave me? Love, Bright

I deleted that.

Dear Sir:
My name is Bright Camila Shelby. I believe I am your daughter. I
would like to meet you, if possible. Please respond as soon as possible.
Sincerely,
Bright Shelby

"You sent him an email?"

I nodded. "For days, I refreshed my email browser, like, 20 times a day. I checked my spam folder almost as often."

Nothing.

On Day 10, I'd decided to give it up. No more checking email. Some people didn't want to be found, right? It had been a bad day. I'd sat on my bedroom floor for hours, who knows how long, watching the razor blade slide up and down my forearms as if someone else were wielding it. I'd cut myself so much so that I'd been nauseous from blood loss. I remember wrapping my arms in towels, walking right behind Kent as he sat staring at the TV, getting more clean towels from the laundry room. He never saw me. I woke up in bloody sheets, hating myself more than ever.

The next day, my dad had showed up in an email.

Dear Bright:
It is true. I'm your father, and a lousy one. Please forgive me.
Dad

CHAPTER 30

On the Blue Ridge

When I had the energy to sit up, I scooped handfuls of water into my mouth. It didn't taste good, but it was water and I desperately needed it. My fall in the water had left me with a few open gashes, one on each knee and one on an elbow, which were bleeding more than I liked to see. All of my fingernails were torn from grasping at the shore and I had several deep scrapes on my torso where I'd dragged myself over the rocks. I drank more water. I rinsed my cuts in the river as best I could.

Still, I had to keep running. I had to run, even though I was exhausted, because I somehow knew that ignoring the sign from the hawk would be the death of me. My body, at this point, felt weightless, boneless, filled with air. I was almost euphoric, simultaneously drained of all energy and filled with a new drive to keep going. I can't totally explain it, but I felt chosen. Fighting had been taught to me, just like Granny Queen had said, and I felt chosen to survive this: to make it out of the Blue Ridge. I felt as though I could read the signs and symbols being laid out before me, and I wasn't afraid anymore—not even a little bit.

So, I wasn't surprised when I noticed a strange white light in the sky. I had never seen anything like it, although I imagined it might be what the northern lights might look like. I'd read a lot about the northern lights, how they take over the night sky and explode in shades of yellow and pink. I used to guess what it must feel like to see them in person. I'd never imagined feeling like I did right then, though, filled with some sort of golden light myself. I felt like I was inside the sky. There is no other way to describe it. It was only much later, once I'd returned home, that I read about the "spirit lights" on the Blue Ridge that native Cherokees and settlers had reported seeing for the past 800 years. The Cherokee legend explained that the lights were the spirits of fallen warriors and the women they'd left behind. Local authorities dismissed them as ambient light from passing trains and cars, although the lights are often reported even when the roads and tracks are closed to traffic.

I know what I saw, and I know what I felt, so you can guess whose version I believe. The light was outside of me and the light was in me, too. I know it sounds crazy, but in that moment, I knew my ancestors were lined up behind me, before me, above me, their voices a chorus leading me forward: "Go on," they said. "Follow the lights. We're shining them for you."

CHAPTER 31

In Raleigh, After

"I think it started in the hospital, the way I divide time."

Catherine looked at me, saying nothing, waiting for me to go on.

I can't really remember exactly when I started setting the timer on my digital watch (nothing fancy, just a cheap Timex) for 15 minutes and 59 seconds. Not 15 minutes. Not 16. Just 15:59. I'd set the timer before I'd do almost anything. Things I enjoy, like art or running or zoning out on my phone, so I didn't get totally lost in them and forget what needed to be done. Things I hate, like writing a book report or doing math problems or cleaning my bathroom, so that I could push through—less than 16 minutes! you can do it!—until the angry little beep announced that I was finished. It even helped with things I am indifferent about, like folding laundry or watching a mindless reality show.

"I'd tell myself I would do whatever it was until the timer went off. Once it beeped, I could decide to set it again or do something else."

In the hospital, time was white space, white noise. Minutes and hours bled into one another and I'm not sure if that had to do with the drugs they were giving me or the blankness of the walls or the sadness of it all, but I needed the timer to ground me. The noise used to drive some of the girls completely bananas, especially the ones with anxiety ("Would you turn off that fucking siren?" this one girl, Lisa, used to scream at me while pulling at either side of her head as if she was in pain). But it got me through the days.

"The anorexics loved me. They loved how I divided my time neatly, how organized I was. They loved how I looked; how tall and skinny I was."

The starving girls would come up to me, their skin transparent, wide green veins pulsing on their foreheads and their temples, eyes dying inside their sockets, and smile. "Your hair is so pretty," they'd stroke my thick black ponytail first, and then their hands would inevitably rise to their own withered heads.

"Was that the first time your looks had been seen as desirable? How did it feel to be someone people felt drawn to and wanted to be around?" Catherine finally spoke.

"Well, I guess it was confusing. I felt like a fraud, since I didn't have to try to be the things they admired. Some of them thought I was anorexic, at first."

Before I went to the hospital, I used the word "anorexic" to describe the appearance-obsessed cheerleaders at my school. Those shallow mirror-lovers who never walked outside their houses without every hair perfectly in place, their outfits flawless, showing just enough skin.

"I didn't understand until I went into the hospital. There was nothing shallow about the girls with anorexia. They had no interest in their appearances. They wanted to disappear." I was quiet for a minute, waiting for Catherine to ask, "Did you want to disappear, too?" She didn't say anything, though.

"Every starving girl in the hospital had some horrible thing happen to her when she was little, and one of the girls died while I was there."

We'd had a group therapy session right after they'd announced that the girl, Layla, was dead. We had all cried, even me, but the anorexics sat together and held hands with each other like they were in it together. Dying. I mean, they were all just sitting there dying together.

"That must have been hard. I'm sorry."

"Yeah. I guess. But we're all just sitting here dying together, aren't we? All of us."

Catherine had looked at me for a long time, saying nothing. I'd already decided I wasn't going to speak again. I hadn't wanted to justify myself, and I'd suddenly felt so tired. After what felt like an hour, she'd finally said, "We are. And we're also living."

CHAPTER 32

On the Blue Ridge

I'd run for several more miles, although I'd completely lost track of how far I'd gone, and my only gauge of time was the light in the sky. My feet were so painful I wasn't sure how much longer I'd be able to go on. I could tell that blisters had formed and burst as I'd run in my wet shoes. My soaked socks rubbed against the raw skin, biting my feet with each step.

Take off your shoes. Let them dry out for a while.

I sat down near the edge of a dirt trail, afraid to see what condition my feet were in. As soon as I sat, my hamstrings seized up, unused to bending after having been upright for so long. I screamed without meaning to, pounding at my hamstrings with my fists until I could stretch them a little without pain. My eyes were grainy, and my vision blurred. I rubbed them, hoping for clarity.

You've had leg cramps before. Take some deep breaths. Move slowly.

My legs had seized painfully after long runs before. This wasn't something to panic about. I gently stretched out on the ground, my legs before me, and took several deep breaths. I felt better. After massaging my hamstrings for a few moments, I untied my soaked, gray shoelaces and yanked off my prized running shoes; the most expensive article of clothing I owned. I noticed my half-painted, ragged fingernails and laughed a little. Getting that manicure seemed like a cruel joke now.

I laid out my shoes, laces spread, in the sun. My socks were stained red and brown and hinted at the condition of my feet. I peeled the blood- and river-soaked fabric off each foot. As I'd guessed, constellations of bloody blisters covered nearly every surface of my feet—heels, every toe, everywhere. My bare feet stung in the gentle breeze. Even though it hurt, I knew I should leave my feet uncovered for a while and let them dry out a little.

At least your toenail polish still looks pretty good.

I knew I was delirious when this thought made me laugh again. Ahead of me, to the right of the trail, I spotted a cement tunnel just above the ground. It reminded me of one of those tunnels on kids' playgrounds that I'd crawl inside; putting my legs on either wall so I'd feel like a giant. I used to love those. This one, I figured, was probably a drainage ditch or something, but I could crawl inside of it and have a hidden place to rest. The sun was low, it was damp, and I realized I wasn't sure how much longer I could last. I picked my way painfully along the dirt path, wincing with every step, in my bare feet.

The smell inside that tunnel was death. An animal was decaying somewhere nearby, and the stench was overwhelming. I felt as though I might have finally sunk to my lowest point. Was that possible? Was this the absolute bottom? Bloody, limping, and filthy. Barefoot. Covered in cuts and bruises and scratches.

Jesus. Could you sink any lower?

"Don't ask stupid questions," I mumbled aloud.

CHAPTER 33

In Raleigh, Before

"My father left before I was born, but for some reason my mother thought she had to share with me all of the legends of his tribe when I was a kid."

She usually avoided talking about the Cherokee in Kent's presence—I now understand that he was genuinely jealous, but back then I thought there might be something shameful or dirty about my heritage—so she saved stories for bedtime and long rides in the car. I guess she wanted me to be proud of where I'd come from; in some way, proud of the father who abandoned me before I was born. The fact that my dad couldn't be bothered to even meet me, much less raise me, seemed lost on her. She didn't question that I'd want to know about him and, of course, she was absolutely right.

"Maybe it had nothing to do with your father. Maybe it had to do with wanting you to be proud of yourself." Catherine didn't miss a beat.

I shrugged. "Either way, when I was in elementary school, I read all about the Cherokee: my father's tribe, my tribe. Back then, I guessed I was picked on, targeted, singled-out because I came from a long line of persecuted people." Exclusion coursed through my veins, as I'd seen it, and I could do nothing to stop it.

"So, you believed your dad was Cherokee without questioning it? Have you ever seen any documentation of his membership in the tribe? Have you registered?"

Oh, yeah. I know. I should dig into it for a million different reasons. I guess a part of me would rather not see the truth in black and white—whether I really am part Cherokee or not—because I've believed one story my entire life. Part of me can't bear the thought that all of it, the legend of my father, could be untrue. Is that stupid?

"No," I said to Catherine. "I don't know why not. I guess I will."

Catherine looked at me a little skeptically, I thought. She didn't say anything for a few moments.

"The Cherokee are also an intensely spiritual people. An adaptable people who are open and welcoming. A proud people, as I understand it. So, you believed the narrative of persecution instead of the narrative of pride?"

"Back then? Yeah. I did."

CHAPTER 34

On the Blue Ridge

Like a dream, I heard a woman's voice right in my ear; close, breathing hot air on my cheek.

Like a nightmare.

"Bad, Natalie," the voice whispered. "You've been a very bad girl."

The sour smell of her breath. My head felt so heavy with sleep, and yet I knew.

Lorraine. She's found you.

I tried to spring to my feet as quickly as I could, but I was knocked back just as fast. I cried out, clutching the small of my back where I'd landed on something sharp.

Lorraine loomed over me. She held a flashlight, so I could see dark blood crusted the side of her head, turning her frizzy yellow doll-hair brown. I'd made her bleed. I'd caused her pain. Her eyes looked blackened, but I couldn't be sure if it was from injury or lack of sleep or just from the shadows cast on her face by the flashlight. She wore the same volunteer shirt from the relay, stained with dried blood.

The relay. Levi. Kent.

I was suddenly filled with such an overwhelming sadness I very nearly cried out from the pain. Why couldn't I ever just have something good? Why did everything I touch turn to blood and tears? What in the hell was wrong with me?

Lorraine was still as a sick statue, still as a corpse, as she stared at me. She was bent over inside the concrete pipe, unable to stand upright because of its height. I saw the ax, the one I'd first seen in her back seat a million years ago, glinting in her right hand. The stench of death seized my stomach.

"Oh, Natalie. You've been such a bad girl. Now I have to punish you." Her voice was thin and sing-songy; the creepy doll voice from before. She grabbed me by the wrist with her left hand, yanking me through the tube. My head throbbed, and I couldn't stand upright, but my head was no match for the searing pain in both of my bare feet. The smell inside the tunnel was making me sick. Finally, we were outside in the cool night. She gripped my wrist so hard I couldn't feel my fingers.

"How did you find me?" I begged, unable to censor my words.

Lorraine laughed unhappily. "You think you're so smart, honey?" She shook her head hard, once, then twice, like she was shaking out a bad idea. "You think you're smarter than I am? Because you grew up in the city? Because you went to that fancy school?" Her voice got louder and louder, approaching a hysterical pitch.

"You've failed me, Natalie. You're a disappointment." Again, with the violent head-shaking. "You're not the same girl I used to know, that's for sure." She held up the ax, looking at the blade as if seeing it for the first time.

"Those disgusting socks, Natalie, and your running shoes. Not so smart to leave them right by the trail, was it?" She cackled, her baby laugh dripping with bitterness. "Not so smart."

I'd left my shoes and socks in plain view of the road. I'd dropped my guard for one second, after having been so careful since I broke away from Lorraine in the first place. One careless mistake.

This is it, Bright. Time to say your prayers and get ready to see Mom. This time, you're dead.

And just like that, over Lorraine's left shoulder, I saw it: the morning star.

Bright morning stars are rising, day is a-breaking in my soul. You are not going out like this.

"You left me, Natalie," she said in an otherworldly voice. The shrieking baby doll voice was gone, and her eyes didn't appear to be focusing, though she was still staring toward the ax. "You hit me. Why did you do that? Why did you leave me hurt and bleeding like that?"

The glow of her face in the pale light of the morning star, the pale glow of the flashlight, terrified me. She looked like a monster.

Think fast, Bright. Appease her. Get her comfortable.

"I'm so sorry, Mama." I forced myself to cry, which wasn't difficult, even though I was too dehydrated for actual tears. "I didn't know what I was doing. I'd never hurt you on purpose. I think it was ..."

THINK.

"...I think it was these pills they make me take, Mama. The people who stole me from you, I mean. I have to take them every day because they say my brain doesn't work right." The words poured out of my mouth. I paused for a moment, watching Lorraine's every gesture. She was still as a stone.

A long moment passed. There was no movement, no sound, no air. I couldn't tell whether or not I'd made a terrible mistake.

"They make you take pills?" Lorraine's eyes shifted in my direction. She still wore a blank expression. I thought I might have gotten to her, though.

"They put me in a hospital once. They said there was something wrong with me and they had to fix it." I paused, wondering how much further to go. "They strapped me to the bed and made me take pills."

Lorraine roared, hurling her flashlight to the ground. The little-girl giggle and the disturbingly sweet voice were gone again. I didn't know who Lorraine had become, and I was scared. I felt cold sweat prickle under my arms.

"They can do that to me, but not to my Natalie! Never to my Natalie! I won't have it. I'll kill every last one of them."

Her voice was brimming with anger but low and growling. She took a step toward me and I flinched.

"See? See what they've done to you? Scared of your Mama?" She wrapped her arms around me. She smelled of body odor and metal and sweat and mold. She held me in her arms for a long time.

"We're going home now, Natalie."

My heart sank at the word: Home. Back to the cabin. Back to captivity. What were the odds that I'd be able to get away again? I was starving. I hadn't eaten anything in ages.

"Did you bring anything to eat, Mama?" I asked gently, still entirely unsure how to treat the woman in front of me but knowing I had to be careful, so careful.

Lorraine's face seemed to snap back to reality. "Oh, is my little girl hungry?" she cooed in her high-pitched voice. She reached into her orange fanny pack and pulled out a plastic bag, tossing it to me.

"You'll be punished later. Know that. Don't you think you're getting away with that stunt you pulled." Her voice was still sweet, melodious, despite her menacing words.

"I brought your favorite snack. Cashews."

Once again, I was disturbed by the volume of trivia she seemed to know about me. Ripping open the bag, I considered that she might have poisoned the nuts just like she poisoned the water what felt like months before. I was so hungry, though, that I didn't care. I shoved the cashews in my mouth, nearly fainting at the salt and fat as it filled my mouth. Lorraine watched me with wide eyes as I ate handfuls of the nuts.

After I'd finished the bag, I decided it wouldn't hurt anything to ask. What more can she do to me than what she's already planned?

"Mama, we've been apart for so long." I began cautiously. "How do you know so much about me? How did you know cashews are my favorite, or that I'm a runner, or that I'm a vegetarian?" I slowly rose to my feet, stuffing the garbage from the cashews into my hoodie pocket. It was chilly, but I knew once the sun came fully up it would be a warmer day. I could smell it in the air.

"Natalie, let's get into the car and I'll tell you all about it." She smiled, and I noticed how different her face was when she was using her scary doll voice. It turned up at every corner, was lit from the eyes.

Lorraine kept her left hand around my wrist and dragged me to the passenger side of her car. I felt every grain of dirt, every pebble under my bare feet. She shoved me into the seat and fell heavily into the driver's seat, laying the ax across her lap. When she was about to put the key in the ignition, she said, "They did those things to me, too." In the same low, gravelly voice she'd used earlier. "They made me take pills, I mean. They made me go to the hospital." She paused and looked down at her lap. "They never strapped me down, though. That must have been awful."

Lifting her eyes toward me, she suddenly looked decades younger, almost like a child.

"There was nothing wrong with me, and there's nothing wrong with you, either."

Lorraine took a deep breath. "One of the things they made me do was go to see a counselor. A really nice lady. Her name was Catherine." I drew in a sharp breath.

Catherine.

She was there. She had long, brown hair. She was in the waiting room when you came out of your sessions. She was always there.

CALL LOG:
DATE: AUGUST 10
TIME: 8:13 A.M.
CATHERINE M. SONDLER, LCSW

Attempted to contact client three times, leaving three messages on client's voicemail. Contact was prompted by news story seen this morning. According to local news, client's home burned to the ground with client's husband inside the home. Client's husband was killed. According to reports, arson is likely and only one body was found inside the home. The news source stated that client could not be located by police for questioning.

CHAPTER 35

On the Blue Ridge

"She helped me a lot for a while, Catherine did. So much that I didn't need to take those pills anymore." She traced the handle of the ax in her lap. We were still sitting in her car.

"One day, I got to my appointment a little early and I saw you leaving Catherine's office. I couldn't believe it was you, but I knew from the moment I saw you that you were my Natalie." She reached out a hand and placed it on top of mine. I forced myself not to snatch it away.

Stay calm. Keep her talking for now.

"So, I started coming earlier and earlier to my sessions with Catherine. I needed to save you, to bring you back to me, but I had to wait until the right time." My face must have registered the horror I felt, because Lorraine shook her head.

"I was smart. I paid attention. One time, on your way out of the session you threw something in the trash can. It was a boarding pass from a flight to Texas."

Austin. That trip Aunt Laura and I took for my last birthday. We heard Sarah Jarosz perform at the Moody Theater and ate tons of Mexican food and I went for a run around the lake. Austin. I loved it. I always thought I'd go back there.

"Another time, a grocery list fell out of your jacket pocket and I read it."

A boarding pass? A grocery list? Catherine's office?

"Well, I may have pulled it out of your pocket when you left your jacket in the waiting room. And if I tell the truth, there was more." She smiled sheepishly, and I tried to keep the disgust from coloring my face. "Once or twice, I followed you when that man picked you up from your appointment—"

"My stepdad." I interrupted. "Followed me? Where did we go?"

She giggled sweetly. "Oh, you know. Different places. Does it matter?"

She followed you. She read your information. She stalked you.

"It sure as hell matters." I couldn't help myself.

I'd barely finished the sentence before I felt the wooden handle of the ax slam across my cheek. The pain stunned me, leaving my left ear ringing. Even though I'd figured it was coming, the hit knocked me off balance for a moment. I shook my head, hoping to clear it.

Calm down, Bright. Keep it together if you want to get out of this alive.

"Sorry, Mama." I muttered.

She still looked put out. "Well, enough of all this. Let's go home." She turned the key in the ignition and a low whirring escaped from the car. Then nothing. She turned it again and the car made no sound at all, just a click as the key turned.

"Darn it!" She shouted, startling me. "Darn it, darn it, darn it!" She pounded her fists on the steering wheel and wrenched her face into a grimace.

This is your chance.

"I can't believe this! The car won't start!" She turned to look at me like this was somehow my fault. "What are we supposed to do now, huh? What are we supposed to do now???" She looked hysterical.

This is a gift. Borrow time. Lie. Whatever you do, do not go back to that cabin.

Die first.

"I know a little bit about cars," I lied, looking at her beseechingly. "Will you pop the hood for me?" I had no clue what to look for, what to do, once she popped the hood, but I needed to stall for as long as I could.

"So, that *stepdad*," she snarled the word, "taught you something after all, huh? Go ahead and take a look." She leaned down to pull the lever to raise the hood and looked at me a little suspiciously but remained behind the wheel of the car. I guessed she assumed that there was nowhere for me to run, out here.

"Don't even think of running off, by the way," she said in her sing-songy voice. "I've got a million different ways to stop you if you do." She paused. "You ain't got your shoes on, anyway. Wouldn't get far, would you?" Hysterical doll laugh.

I shook my head and began fumbling under the hood of the hatchback. It just looked dark and dirty under there, not that I would have any idea what I was looking for anyway.

"I need a flashlight. And do you have any tools?" I shouted over the hood, another stalling technique. "Like, a tool kit for emergencies?" Lorraine sighed heavily and climbed out of the car. She opened the hatchback and pulled out a nondescript black case.

"Not sure what all is in there, but something might help." She passed the heavy case to me. I noticed that she seemed a little unsteady on her feet. What exactly had my smack with the pot done to her? This was good news.

I popped open the case and surveyed its contents. Wrench, some mysterious metal screws with an unclear purpose, blah, blah…and a tire iron. Without even thinking I slid the iron up the sleeve of my hoodie. I steadied my breathing.

Just keep going. Don't arouse suspicion. Just keep going.

I found a flashlight and flicked it on, pretending to tinker under the hood for a little while longer. "Mama, will you try the ignition again?" She turned the key and, unsurprisingly, nothing happened.

"Darn it." I pretended to be frustrated. "I'm not sure what else to do."

I watched as Lorraine got out of the vehicle and walked slowly toward me. Unsure what she planned to do, I stood still, one hand on the car and one on the black case, ever mindful of the tire iron up my sleeve. She had her flashlight in one hand and the ax in the other.

She shone the light in my face, blinding me, and I flinched.

"What are you up to, Missy?" She cooed, continuing to shine the light at me. "Huh? You up to something? You think your ol' mama's a dummy, do ya?" She lifted the ax slowly to my throat, holding it awkwardly high on the handle, the blade grazing my skin.

"Do you think I'm stupid, Natalie? Huh?" She pressed the blade into my neck a little and it stung. I drew in a sharp breath. "Because I'm not stupid."

I exhaled. "I don't think you're stupid. I don't. I just can't fix the car." I was terribly aware of the tire iron in my sleeve. I couldn't go after her with the tire iron while she was still holding the ax, though. I couldn't move, couldn't really breathe, without her slicing my neck with the blade.

"Mama, will you please lower the ax?" I asked in as innocent a voice as I could muster. "You're hurting me." Lorraine glared at me for a moment before something appeared to snap in her face, like she'd suddenly recognized me. She lowered the ax and turned away from me.

"Here." She pulled a bandana out of her jeans pocket. "You're bleeding." I pressed the bandana to my neck and saw that she was right—it darkened and, even though there was not much light outside, I could tell that it was wet with my blood.

You've gotta get out of here. Ten more minutes and you'll be dead.

"Mama, it's really getting late. I think we should just plan to stay here until daylight. Don't you?" I said it casually, like I wasn't invested in her response at all.

She nodded almost imperceptibly. "I guess you're right. We can sleep in the car." She looked me up and down as I climbed in. "You'll stay in the front seat, Missy. And you should know that I'm an incredibly light sleeper."

In that moment, I made my decision.

The nerves in my fingers were suddenly alive; they burned as I clenched my hand tighter.

What do you know about hurting anybody? You really think you've learned how to fight?

"Mama, I really need to use the bathroom. I've got nowhere to go, and I don't want to run anyway." I put my hand on her shoulder, even though it disgusted me to do it. "I don't even have any shoes on." Lorraine was slumped over a little, staring at the ground.

"I can tell you're not feeling your best. You stay here. I'll go right outside. If I'm not back in two minutes, you come for me, okay?"

Unbelievably, Lorraine grunted her permission, holding the ax in one hand, the flashlight in the other.

I stepped away from the car and forced myself to think fast. A shiver trailed down my back, between the wings of my shoulders. I knelt. I was a spring, coiled tightly behind some brush. I could hear my heartbeat and feel the rocky earth underneath my bare feet.

"Hurry." Lorraine's high voice had sounded like sickness, like wheezing. She'd barked out a cough.

Now, as dry branches scraped my knees and I tasted blood on my lips, I was diseased by my thoughts:

What if you can't? What if you miss? What if you fail?
What if you haven't learned?

The tire iron was cold underneath my right thigh. It was heavy enough, I guessed, but I wouldn't know its true weight until I raised it over my head, ready to strike. Then, there would be no turning back and nothing left to do but run. I could only guess which way to head next. I felt so tired, so incredibly weary from everything I'd been through. I started to doubt my sanity.

Your ancestors are lined up behind you. The Blue Ridge holds you in its hand. The sky has lined itself with stars. Take your chance.

"What are you doing back there?" her voice again, thick like her ax. "Get back here right now."

I rose to my tiptoes, still in a crouch. My legs felt strong. She'd gotten out of the car and was coming toward me.

Now.

With every ounce of my will, I raised the iron over my head and smashed it over hers. I don't remember doing it, really. I just know I didn't connect with her; I swung ferociously at the air. I remember the breathlessness I felt afterward, tossing the iron somewhere behind me and sprinting away from the car.

And then I tripped, and she was over me, her face a sweaty moon above mine. She didn't look human, spittle flying out of her mouth and her hands—so strong—pressing down on my neck.

Breathe, Bright. Breathe.

I couldn't get any air in my windpipe, and I willed myself not to panic. Suddenly, I was furious. Angrier than I'd ever been in my entire life. Filled with a white-hot rage that I'd never felt before. I'd lived through so much, survived all of it, and I wouldn't allow things to end like this.

I reached up and pried her hand off my neck, simultaneously landing a knee in her stomach. She grunted and lunged back at me as I growled, "Who in the hell do you think you are?"

My voice tore open the sky, driven by fury I'd never believed possible. I didn't have any leverage, but I kicked at her anyway with every bit of strength I could muster. She roared.

"Just who in the hell do you think you are?" I repeated, and she wailed, "I'm your mottthhhhhher…" as I smacked the side of her face with my fist. I had to get off the ground if I was going to survive this, but I was in such an awkward position.

"My mother? My mother died ten years ago! God…you? You're nothing! You destroy life, you don't make it! You're a killer! Go to hell!"

On my last word, I shoved both of Lorraine's shoulders as hard as I could, thrusting her backward into the darkness. In a moment, I was on my feet.

"RRRRRAAAAAHHHHHHHHHH!" She flew at me like a wild animal, but I could tell her strength was waning. Blood poured from her nose—did I do that?—and she was hunched over as she ran, as if her stomach was in pain.

The razor blade. Use the razor blade in your pocket.

How could I have forgotten? I felt like I was moving in slow motion as I dug in my key pocket and frantically unwrapped the blade. Everything stood still. I couldn't feel my fingers or my hands, but I knew the blade was there.

You never used it. Not once during this entire nightmare. You never even thought of it.

I jammed it into the side of her neck as hard as I could, not even caring if I cut my own fingers in the process. She fell backward, out of my sight, with a sick gurgle.

There was nothing but buzzing in my ears—that buzz that often accompanies a fainting spell—but I turned and ran. I kept running. I knew that was the only option I had. I didn't think about what I had just done, I only thought about going, spreading distance again, getting out of there as fast as my bare feet could take me.

I'd fought. Somehow, I knew I was going to make it.

I didn't know how much time had passed when two men appeared out of nowhere, a few yards apart in the narrow dirt lane. Drawing closer, I realized it was the quilt of fog which had obscured them, and their sudden presence pumped my legs with adrenaline. My feet were in so much pain that they'd gone numb, and I could tell I was hobbling more than running, but I kept going. I ran faster toward the two, each step carrying me inches closer to home.

Home. The word felt like a lifetime gone. Now, my temples throbbing and my blood thick from dehydration, I couldn't be sure how long I'd been in these woods. As I ran, the two figures sharpening with the closing distance, I imagined my homecoming; to Kent, to school, to Glenlake. I imagined my stepfather greeting me in the newspaper-littered foyer, his eyes papery in the corners and shot through with red, his shirt crumpled from late nights and tense phone calls, his cuticles bitten raw. Aunt Laura would be there, too, gold bracelets clicking up her arms as she trapped me in her embrace. *"We are so glad you're home,"* Aunt Laura would sigh into my ear, crying quietly. *"We haven't closed our eyes since you disappeared."*

And what about school, I wondered? What had the kids at school made of my absence? Had they counted me as a casualty or a runaway? Had they thought I was back in the psych ward? Had they thought of me at all? I was acutely aware that, while I never thought I cared about being missed, I'd daydreamed about it. Imagining Kent, Aunt Laura, Brenda, my teachers, my classmates…imagining their thoughts trained on my absence, their prayers aimed at my safe return; picturing them hanging urgently lettered signs on the community mailboxes around Glenlake, I was mortified to admit even to myself that this felt good. I liked the fantasy of their regret.

Considering this, I realized I was now ten steps away from the men. In an instant, I also realized that they were not two men, after all. One was, stout and black-haired, and one was a girl who might have been about my age. As I neared them, I tried to get their attention.

"Hey!" My voice was strangled, dry from lack of use.

"Hey!" I tried again, "Could you please—I need some help…hey." Each word weighed a hundred pounds, stuck in my throat. I tried to raise my arms for emphasis, noting that the man and the girl just stared at me in silence.

Whether caused by fog or dehydration, I couldn't be sure, but I couldn't keep either face in focus. Each shifted and bloated, frightening me. I stopped running. I looked up at the sky. I could've sworn I saw two giant, graceful wings gliding over my head, blocking out the light.

"Please help me," I muttered one last time, right before the world went dark.

CHAPTER 36

On the Blue Ridge

My mouth tasted like metal. I couldn't ever remember a feeling in my mouth like that before—such an intense thirst, such a chemical taste, such a pain between where my eyes and the back of my skull intersected. My mouth tasted like a thousand deserts, like a hundred breaths, like no water, like never going home. I knew I was crying, but I still had no tears.

I was aware of only two things: the intense pain in my head and a sudden overwhelming sadness that seemed to emanate from somewhere in the middle of my chest. Look, I'm familiar with sadness. I've known it for most of my life. We're connected. At times, I've even felt as though sadness were my only friend. But that day felt different. That sadness felt less like an outfit I was wearing and more like my skin. It suddenly felt like I was never going to be home again.

I couldn't see anything, just the blackness beyond my eyes. Had I been blinded? Would it even be worth it to be rescued? I flashed back to those first moments Lorraine led me to the cabin, a black bag covering my face. How long ago had that been? It felt like years. I felt myself lifted and briefly wondered if I was already dead and if my spirit might be leaving my body.

"Está enferma," the voice said loudly. *She's sick.*

"Bueno, ¿qué vas a hacer?" A girl's voice. Afraid. *What are you going to do?*

"Vamos al hospital. Ella necesita ayuda y nosotros podemos ayudarla, gracias a Dios."

And with those words, *She needs help and we can help her, thank God,* I exhaled. I was suddenly warm and comfortable. I thought I might be in a bed, and I was covered in a blanket. I wanted to pass out, then heard an upbeat Tejano song filter through the car radio.

Keep it together, Bright. You haven't come this far to black out now.

Though I couldn't see and couldn't speak, I could listen. I forced myself to listen to the music until it morphed into something familiar.

And then, like an angel, Alison Krauss sang to me.

"As I went down to the river to pray…"

Just stay awake until the end of the song. Just until the song ends. You can even sing along if you want.

The pair in the front seat murmured quietly in Spanish, perhaps aware that I could hear them.

"Oh, sisters, let's go down, let's go down, come on down," Alison and I sang.

I imagined Alison above me, angel wings wide as the sky, smiling down at me.

Stay awake until the song ends.

Stay alive until the song ends.

The Spanish whispering continued as I felt the vehicle slow. Again, without my awareness or consent, I felt myself lifted.

"Good Lord, show me the way..."

The music faded, and I heard the truck pull away. The world went black once more.

CHAPTER 37

On the Blue Ridge

They'd taken me to the emergency room, the dark-haired man and the teenaged girl. They rolled their truck up to the ER's entrance. They lifted my body out of the truck and laid me gently right by the entrance door. And that is how the ER nurse found me.

My body was a wreck. I had a severe concussion, several torn ligaments, a surface cut on my neck from the ax, infected blisters on both of my feet, and a wound on my forehead. I had to be treated for dehydration and with charcoal to counteract the poison Lorraine had given me. And those were just the physical effects. My first thoughts were of Kent, waking up in that hospital bed. And the first person I saw, as I opened my eyes, was Kent.

He looked ten pounds thinner and five years older, though I'd only been gone four days. His skin was loose around his eyes and his stubble had grown out. I couldn't control my sobs when I saw him. I couldn't stop.

"Oh, Brighty." He put both hands on my shoulders as I sat propped up in that hospital bed; IV fluids dripping into one arm. This was a different hospital than the one where I'd healed from my burns. I was a different person. So was he.

"I thought you were gone." His voice broke on the last word. He shook his head, trying to regain his composure. Embarrassed. "I can't believe I let you go like that."

He paused, breathing in. "I can't believe I haven't been better. For you."

Still sobbing, those words stopped me in my tracks. "What?"

"I let you down, Bright." He couldn't look me in the eye, instead focusing on the gauze-thin blanket draped over my knees. "I haven't been the father you've needed. I know that." He rubbed one eye with his fist. Was he trying to pretend he wasn't crying? Weren't we so far past that now?

"What?" It was all I could say. I couldn't think. I was stunned. Thrilled and devastated all at once.

"I'm going to do better." He stepped back from the bed a few inches. "Not just for you, but for your mother—"

"Kent," I interrupted, my throat dry, "This wasn't your fault."

He fell backward into the mint green hospital chair heavily, closing his eyes for a little longer than a blink. My words knocked him over.

"Not this," he said, "but losing you forever would have been."

I swallowed hard. Sweat was beading on my upper lip even though the room was cool. I was suddenly conscious of my smell: a revolting mixture of body odor, metal, and rubbing alcohol. *Losing me forever,* he'd said. I could have been lost forever. I managed not to get lost forever.

Me.

Why is this so hard?

This isn't hard.

"You can't lose me." I said the words slowly, not even sure exactly what I was about to say, but knowing my words were true. I felt dizzy; almost euphoric. Butterflies in my stomach.

"You and me, we belong to each other." Did this even make sense? "You've never left me. You're the dad I've always needed, and I love you."

Maybe I'd said those words years before. Maybe I'd told Kent I loved him when I was little. But I couldn't remember telling him, and I needed to speak the truth to him right then. Even though it hurt to say the words, I needed to let him know.

Kent was still as a stone, but tears poured from his eyes. "You know, Brighty, all I've ever really wanted is for you to be happy." He stopped talking to take in a deep breath. "I'd even pray to God, a God I'm not too sure about, 'Please, just let her be happy. Give her real happiness.' I thought it was just about being happy, getting through this life."

He stopped talking for a long moment. So long, really, that I thought he might be done. I couldn't look at him because my chest hurt. It was hard, but it was the good kind of hard.

"It's taken this," he waved his hands over the hospital bed, "to know I shouldn't be wishing for your happiness."

I looked at him, surprised.

"I should've stopped wishing a long time ago. You're so strong. I should have just seen your strength."

You're strong.

You belong.

You learned to fight.

. . .

Finn, NC—After an extensive 52-hour search, a Raleigh teen who went missing in the forest west of Courtney during an ultra-relay race has been found alive.

Seventeen-year-old Bright Shelby was running the annual North Carolina Mountain Relay race with five teammates when they say she went out for her first leg of the race, a 14-mile road and trail run, at about 9 p.m. Saturday and never arrived at the relay checkpoint.

"These woods are thick, and she isn't from around here," said Sgt. Cole Martinez of the Baxter County Sheriff's Office. "Her team looked for her in their van, but a lot of the course is on trails where the van can't go. Her team contacted the race director, who eventually called the sheriff's office at about 11:30 on Saturday night."

Explorer scouts with Baxter County worked with the sheriff's office and other searchers overnight to attempt to locate her.

At some point before dawn on Monday morning, two unidentified adults discovered Shelby and brought her anonymously to the Baxter County Emergency Room. Any information on Shelby's rescuers should be forwarded to the sheriff's department. Details are still unfolding about what happened to Shelby, but sources say she was abducted from the relay course and held captive in the woods.

Approximately 150 volunteers searched for the teen, including search and rescue personnel.

It is believed she was within 100 yards of areas checked by rescue workers and volunteers, but due to the heavily wooded area, visibility was extremely difficult.

CHAPTER 38

In Raleigh, After

Now that I've been back home for a year, things are different. Not perfect. There's less of an edge to my days—there's less pain getting out of bed in the morning. There are more moments when I'm able to stop and take deep breaths. I can close my eyes now and not see Lorraine. I sleep through the night and run early in the morning before the sunrise.

I've done so much talking; so much work. I've learned a lot. I've learned there's a universe inside of me. I've also learned what doesn't belong to me. I know I'm not irreparably damaged, too broken, or filled with too much darkness for anyone else to handle. I can unhook from my past and from my old beliefs. A new day always comes. I can wait for it or work through it or stay silent or be afraid of it, but, I've learned, that new day will still come, just like it did when I was on the Blue Ridge.

I've learned that one reason I hurt myself was because I couldn't tolerate my feelings, and one of the most intolerable feelings for me was that of not being good enough. I thought I should've arrived on this earth already complete. I thought I should have things figured out, wrapped up and tied with a shiny ribbon. But there aren't neat bows on anything, because nothing's finished yet. It helps that Kent and I see Catherine together about once a month. We are working on staying accountable to one another. We are working on feeling, even when it hurts. Some days it's like running through mud. Other days are better. Watching Kent struggle reminds me that so many of us must be taught how to fight. It doesn't come naturally to him, either, but he's brave.

Kent's even started going on short runs with me sometimes. I've already noticed how his mood shifts when he's outside in the fresh air, moving through space. He makes fun of his pace, his form, his age…but he loves it and so do I.

I don't know what it means to grow up Native American in those traditions, steeped in culture, taught all the ways of the Cherokee. I know I can choose to either live high or I can be someone who feels angry for what I missed. I can believe in magic and I can make my own magic. I can say thanks every day for the rising sun and the coffee that's hot and the water flowing from my shower, and I am more likely to do that today than I was before. I don't understand everything, but I understand some things far better than I did before I was lost and found on the Blue Ridge. I know that even if I don't have any company in a given moment, I always have myself. I got comfortable with being alone when I was on the Blue Ridge, and I've realized that I can be pretty good company.

I still run by myself, in the preserve. There, I can get quiet and hear the rustle of the pines, the lull of the wind, the crunch of the fallen leaves. There, I'm reverent. I feel all my body's cells, imagining them working together to move me through the air. Sometimes, I make music in my head, knitting together the sounds I love. Now more than ever, I know my time on earth is limited, so I'm trying to make it beautiful. I'm trying to appreciate its beauty, too—a certain D7 guitar chord, a lavender sweater, the stars. I don't have to own things to appreciate them; the stars don't have to belong to me, even though I think they do, just a little bit. I don't have to own the music, or the boy, or the life, to value it. I don't have to have my mom in this world to love her. I can't possess people— not Levi, not Brenda. But I can hold them in my heart even when they aren't in my life. All I need is my mind, my soul, my strong body, the great sky, and the music in my head. The world is enormous and complicated and filled with every kind of sorrow. It will break my heart. But I'd rather let the world break my heart than continue breaking my own skin.

Catherine is my life support lately. She reminds me to keep breathing on the tough days, and she keeps showing me the beauty of the world, especially when it's hard to see. Most days, I feel pretty okay. Some days it's more than that.

If I were reading this, I'd probably want to know about Levi. We keep in touch. We're friends. But this was never a story that was going to end with the two of us in love, was it? He's too free-spirited and open-hearted for someone like me, but we sure do love to run together. We've seen each other a few times since the relay, and we hit the trails and never run out of things to talk about. He and I will always be connected.

So, there's no Levi, but maybe someday there will be someone else. For now, I am content. I'm getting to know myself and falling in love with the world that's always been just beyond my awareness. I'm taking a year to work before I decide about college, and I plan to spend some of it exploring. I just scheduled a trip to go see the northern lights, and after that I might go back to Austin. Alison Krauss is performing a few dates in Nashville, and I'd like to spend some time running the trails around Percy Priest Lake while I'm there. I hear it's beautiful.

And Lorraine. The truth is, for a few days I thought I'd killed her. I didn't feel the slightest bit satisfied with that outcome, though. Maybe that's because when it comes down to it, if I look at what happened as honestly as I can, Lorraine and I really aren't that different. She had problems that led her to hurt people, and so did I. She escaped from a world that was too painful to bear, just like I did. She had people who loved her and people who abandoned her, she had talents and failures, she had Catherine. Her reality and mine collided for a reason, and I know that now. I'm glad I didn't kill her. I hope she gets the help she needs. I hope she never hurts anyone ever again, although I'm not sure I can ever forgive her for killing Flyer.

I petitioned her judge for leniency on both my charges and the charges in Eddie's murder case. I spoke in front of the courtroom, asking how anyone could be held accountable for crimes they committed when they were deeply, intractably mentally ill. The judge's eyes were blank as he gazed back at me—I couldn't read his face.

"Miss Shelby, why are you speaking on behalf of Miss Meyer? In your own words."

I was caught off guard.

"She made my life hell for a few days," I said, "but her life was hell for years. She needs treatment, not prison time. She needs help."

He nodded, his face registering no emotion.

The crush of everything; the crush of my mother dying, of my loneliness, of my overwhelming emotions. I used to think the torrent of all this was why I was going to give up and fall apart. Now, I think the crush has led to the fight. The only way not to be crushed is to get stronger, like the gardeners who make their plants tougher by exposing them, bit by bit, to increasingly damaging elements. Granny Queen was right all those years ago. Because I didn't learn to fight, it was taught to me. I had to go to the Blue Ridge to learn how to overcome the crush, how to fight back, how to fight for myself, how to fight for others. Without Lorraine, I would've died under the weight of it all. I had to learn to stop backing down, curling in, collapsing under the weight. I had to run toward the stars, not away from them.

I know I was prepared for all of this; honed for it. I was conceived out of fire and burned over and over and over again. I understood pain; I welcomed it. My escape out had to be a journey through. It wouldn't have worked otherwise.

Now, I keep writing it out, over and over, like a mantra or a wish or song lyrics or a dream I don't want to forget. I keep writing it and rewriting it and I'm not even really sure I'll ever get it right.

The voice in my head hasn't completely disappeared. It's still there, but I'm usually able to shut it up when I need to. I don't want to shut it up entirely, after all. It helped me. It kept me running.

Once, Catherine told me to picture myself as a baby when I'm having a hard time being kind to myself. To talk to myself with love as if I were a little child. Love, that's the way to live your life. That's the way I'm choosing to go forward from this point. My biological dad may decide to be a part of it or he may not. The dad I've always needed, who would never harm me or abandon me, is the central person in my world. Without Kent, I'd never really understand everything I went through. He's my skeleton. He holds me up.

Most of the time, Catherine is my voice. She's helped me articulate so many things I never thought I'd say. She's molded words around these shapeless feelings and handed me a pen and paper and whispered, "Write."

Levi was my lungs. He gave me breath when I needed it, his friendship gives me breath now. I might never have joined the relay team if it wasn't for him. This thought occurred to me more than once. And who would I have been if I had never been through this experience? Who would I be without that suffering? What if I'd never been taught how to fight?

My heart is mine, but so many others live there. My mother does, and Kent, and even my biological father, too. My brain may tell me that she shouldn't, but Lorraine also occupies a small corner of my heart. Right or wrong, she's there.

When I walked into Catherine's office this Monday, exactly a year from the day Kent and I pulled up to the Mountain Inn for the relay, I was wearing a sleeveless top. Catherine had never seen me without sleeves, and when she saw me her eyes went wide behind her glasses, just for a second. Surprise opened her face like a present. In the next moment, she smiled. Though she's never tried to hug me in all this time, I got the feeling she wanted to. Instead, she put her hand to her own chest as if checking the beat of her heart. I could swear her eyes were welling up with tears, but when she spoke, I heard none in her voice.

"Bright," she said, "they are beautiful."

And just like that, everything fell away. She was right, of course: My arms are beautiful; made new, transformed by a tattoo artist's needle into canvases of gold and burnt sienna, each hawk feather painstakingly outlined and filled in, injured and then healed, now unfolded for the world to see. Each one of my scars is still there, underneath the elaborate wings. The evidence of what I've survived, what I've learned, is underneath the beauty. My scars won't go anywhere. But I'm in charge of my own transformation, of creating my own art. I've learned how to fight. I'm not hiding from it anymore: My pain has become my wings.

About the Author

Anne Wakefield worked as a clinical social worker for nearly two decades, publishing short stories and articles while she wrote her first novel. A native Texan, Anne spent ten formative years in North Carolina before returning to Austin with her husband, two sons, and two dogs. Follow her on Instagram at @arwakefield_writer for updates.

Made in the USA
San Bernardino, CA
02 September 2018